His Christmas Pride

Renée Dahlia

16pt

Read How You Want
LARGE PRINT BOOKS, BRAILLE & DAISY

Copyright Page from the Original Book

 ESCAPE publishing

TABLE OF CONTENTS

His Christmas Pride Renée Dahlia   ii

About the author   v

Acknowledgements   vi

Chapter 1   1

Chapter 2   9

Chapter 3   16

Chapter 4   23

Chapter 5   35

Chapter 6   48

Chapter 7   60

Chapter 8   80

Chapter 9   99

Chapter 10   110

Chapter 11   125

Chapter 12   134

Chapter 13   146

Chapter 14   167

Chapter 15   174

Epilogue   185

Bestselling Titles by Escape Publishing...   193

His Christmas Pride Renée Dahlia

Sam Viravaidya knows he's thrown his brother Kiet under the bus by asking him to deliver oysters from their farm to a Rainbow Cove Christmas lunch. But his ex-girlfriend will be there and Sam would rather not see her. She broke it off because he needed to 'grow up'. He suspects she's right, but he also knows he'd much rather hang out online in SkyDiscHooks creating cities and chatting to the mysterious Velebit. Being an adult is overrated, and so is Christmas. When his friendship with Velebit grows into something more, Sam doesn't need to worry about serious. Velebit lives on the other side of the world ... doesn't he?

When Sam discovers Velebit is actually Mick, the local paramedic, he could not be more surprised.

After a devastating factory fire, Mick has fled the city and just wants to settle down to a quiet country life. When Mick discovers his online crush lives nearby, and is just as gorgeous in real life, he's hooked. But Mick isn't convinced Sam will stick around for him, and he's not ready to risk his heart. Will Sam be able to grow up in

About the author

RENÉE DAHLIA is an unabashed romance reader who loves feisty women and strong, clever men. Her books reflect this, with a side-note of dark humour. Renée has a science degree in physics. When not distracted by the characters fighting for attention in her brain, she works in the horse-racing industry doing data analysis and writing magazine articles. When she isn't reading or writing, Renée wrangles a partner and four children, volunteers on the local cricket club committee, and is the Secretary of Romance Writers Australia.

If you'd like to know more about Renée, her books, or to connect with her online, you can:
visit her webpage www.reneedahlia.com
follow her on twitter https://twitter.com/dekabat
or like her Facebook page https://www.facebook
.com/reneedahliawriter/.

Acknowledgements

I acknowledge the Wangal people of the Eora Nation, who are the traditional custodians of the land on which this book was written. I also acknowledge the Gumbaynggirr Nation, where Rainbow Cove is fictionally located. I pay my respects to the Elders past and present.

Thank you to the team at Escape: Nicola Robinson, Johanna Baker, my copy editor Linda Nix, and the rest of the team at Harlequin who pulled this novel into a book. Thanks also to the Rainbow Cove writing team, and to Lina the plot-solving champion.

To online friends: your friendship is real.

When I was chatting to a queer friend about this book, she said, 'You have to end it at Mardi Gras, that's like gay Christmas.' And so, this ending is for you, Deb.

Chapter 1

Sam carried the cooler box of oysters from the packing shed and placed them into the Rainbow Cove Oyster Farm van. He'd been out on the boat early this morning, with the sunrise shimmering gold and orange on the water, to harvest oysters for his friend Christophe's Christmas lunch today. He picked the nicest ones he could find this morning, since he couldn't attend ... *for reasons, coughs* ... Sam shook his head slightly. He obviously spent too much time online if he was starting to think in online chat phrasing. Not that he'd admit that to his older brother, Kiet.

'Thanks. Or no thanks?' Kiet shut the van doors, turned to him, and gave him a long-suffering look.

Sam held up his hands. 'I know. I know. I should be the one going to this party, after all, it's my friends.' They'd been arguing about this for a couple of weeks, basically since Sam sprung it on Kiet.

'I told you not to sleep with her. Sex complicates everything, and now she's been stealing from us, and has done the bolt.'

Sam crossed his arms over his chest. 'Okay, some of that is not true. Lizzy hasn't run off.

She'll be at Christophe's Christmas party. That's why I don't want to go.'

'You should go. She might listen to you, and we can find out what happened to our money.'

Sam huffed out a breath. 'Firstly, I don't believe that Lizzy stole from us. She wouldn't.' He ignored Kiet's sneer. 'And secondly, she broke up with me. I'm, like, the last person she'll talk to now.' Apparently, Lizzy thought he needed to grow up, stop playing games online, and be more manly. She hadn't exactly said it in those words. It was more that he felt the accusation because it was a familiar one. There were plenty of times growing up in this town when he'd been bullied for not being manly enough, or rather, not being blokey enough. He'd lashed out when Lizzy mentioned it, perhaps unfairly, but still, she had to have known it would hurt him. Being bisexual meant he apparently gave off gay vibes—whatever that meant—to his bogan classmates, who threw in a bit of racism thanks to his Thai father, so he was super glad Kiet had sent him to boarding school in Sydney for the last two years of high school. He wasn't sure he'd have survived another couple of years at Marandowie High. But he had survived, and he'd come back to town and made friends—friends who were having a party that he wanted to avoid because Lizzy would also be there. It was a mess.

'Fine. I'll go. Christophe is the farm's client. We can't disappoint him, and I'll see if I can work out what the hell Elizabeth's motivations are.' Kiet held up one hand. His determination to call Lizzy by her full name irritated Sam. 'Stop. Before you defend her, you have to see that the timing sucks. Just as we notice someone has been stealing from the business, she breaks up with you and quits her job.'

'It's a coincidence.' Things between him and Lizzy had been tense for ages. Working and living together, especially in the tiny cottage he and Kiet called home, wasn't a recipe for success. He and Lizzy bickered a lot, so it shouldn't have come as a surprise that she had been searching for a new job for months now. That she kept sleeping with him during that time was a boon to his ego—the sex was good enough to stay for—but apparently it wasn't enough for Lizzy. Even with all of that, he refused to believe she was behind the missing money. She was too honest to steal from them. Brutally honest at times, hence they'd broken up.

'Whatever. I'll find the truth.' Kiet walked over and thumped Sam on the shoulder, the same way he always said goodbye, then jumped in the van and drove off with a spin of the wheels on the gravel driveway. Sam waited until the van had disappeared down the long driveway and turned onto the road before he let himself relax.

The relief at not having to go to Christophe's party was huge, and he pushed away the stab of guilt from sending Kiet in his place. His conscientious big brother wasn't the best at socialising, and Sam knew he only had a couple of hours to himself before Kiet made an excuse to avoid people. He'd be back at the farm soon enough, and they could have a couple of beers together on the decrepit porch overlooking the oyster farm. The view over Rainbow Cove was stunning. Sam would never tire of it. He'd missed it when he'd gone away to finish his schooling, then years at university gaining his science degree in aquaculture, and a Masters degree with a thesis in an incredibly niche area of oyster farming.

He strode back to the cottage to grab a snack and sit down at his laptop for a break. With all the drama lately, he hadn't logged into his Sky Disc Hooks account for a few days, and he missed it. The online game had everything—chat groups with people from all over the world, including his cousins in Thailand—and enough strategy to make playing the actual game fun. The game was a nod to Terry Pratchett's Discworld, and Sam had built his own disc with his own city and farms. Lately he'd been trading with the user Velebit. Velebit had been on SDH for a while before Sam googled his username out of curiosity. It was a mountain range in Croatia, so he assumed Velebit lived near there. After all, his username, Crassostrea, was the Latin name for oysters.

After grabbing a snack, Sam sat down and logged in, careful not to get crumbs near his keyboard. The lack of available time to himself before Kiet came home again meant he broke his usual rule of not eating near his keyboard. A new shipment of platinum had arrived. Sweet. He fiddled around for a while in the game, shifting a few things, and finishing the build of his latest trading shed. Better this than a party with people he'd gone to school with and hadn't been sensible enough to leave town for good. Sam rolled his neck on his shoulders—he wasn't usually so cynical; he'd stayed and for his own good reasons. Others might have their reasons too. Maybe he should've gone to the party. It might have been nice to chat to a few people, have a beer or two, and enjoy some of Christophe's amazing food. Well ... it wasn't Christmas yet in the rest of the world, there might be a few people online to chat with, and of course, loads of countries didn't celebrate Christmas. His Thai cousins would most likely be around at some point during the day. The internet was so great for keeping in touch with friends and relatives who lived overseas. He clicked on the messages icon to see a note from Velebit.

Velebit: Any plans for all that platinum? A little dot flashed to indicate Velebit was currently online.

Crassostrea: I could trade some.

Velebit: Or you could give me a xmas pressie?

Crassostrea: Cheeky! Do you celebrate xmas in Croatia? Sam didn't know much about that country, except the capital Dubrovnik was a known party hub. He'd traded with Velebit plenty of times over the last few months, and they'd bantered with each trade, but so far they hadn't ventured into anything personal. Velebit's trades were clever, and the way Velebit applied strategy showed a bit of life experience. Still, there was every chance Velebit was a genius ten-year-old girl. Who could tell on the internet?

Velebit: Croatia?

Crassostrea: Your handle is some mountains from there. I assumed.

Velebit: I was born near there. Came to Australia when I was five.

Sam leaned back in his chair, unsure how to respond. Then: *Crassostrea: I'm an Aussie too.* It didn't really describe everything, but whatever.

Velebit: Cool. Whereabouts?

Crassostrea: Small town.

Velebit: That's a cagey answer for someone curious enough to google my username. ☺

Crassostrea: Lol. Anyway, basic safety. You could be an old white guy seeking out young girls.

The answer took ages to come through. Either Sam had offended Velebit or he was typing out a very long response.

Velebit: Old is relative, I've just turned thirty. Most people would say being Croatian makes me white. And why am I online on xmas day? I have to work later today and I'm filling in time until my shift. What you are doing online on xmas day? Avoiding family?

Sam shook his head. *Crassostrea: It's complicated.*

Velebit: So you're a teen girl who shouldn't be chatting online to a 30yo bloke then?

Crassostrea: You answered white and old, but not guy. If you're a girl, you should be careful.

Velebit: Read above. 30yo bloke. You?

Crassostrea: A bored mid-20s queer bloke who doesn't do xmas. Sam held his breath. Telling someone, even online, that he was queer could go either way. He chuckled at his own bisexual pun, then rolled his eyes at himself. He had no one to share that with, and for all of the arguments he'd had with Lizzy, he missed having someone to share silly jokes with.

Velebit: Makes sense. Hard to meet other gays in a small town. And SDH is basically a queer hook-up joint.

Sam frowned. It was? He'd missed that when he signed up. *Crassostrea: And you know this, how?*

Velebit: Ex-boyfriend introduced me to it back in Sydney.

Crassostrea: Ok.

Velebit: Plus, think about it. The whole game is basically to make your own place on a disc, then 'hook up' with other disc owners to make a bigger city. It's a giant gay pun.

Sam laughed. How had he not noticed that? *Crassostrea: Does that make us two bored queers alone on xmas? How cliched.*

Velebit: rofl

Crassostrea: omg, you are old! Who uses rofl anymore?

Velebit: Mate, when I was born, the internet didn't exist.

Sam opened a new tab and googled. The internet was opened to the public in 1995. *Crassostrea: Are you sure you are only 30?*

Velebit: Unless my father forged my birth certificate! :D Anything is possible.

Chapter 2

Mick hit send on the comment before he could second-guess himself. He didn't usually tell people about his Croatian heritage. Mick had been born during the Yugoslav wars in the early nineties, and his father had PTSD from fighting in various skirmishes. When rumours of ethnic cleansing flowed through the land, they'd abandoned their home and convinced a cousin in Sydney to help them get refugee status.

Crassostrea: Argh, family.

Mick knew it would be easy to say something throw-away, but something in the way Crassostrea wrote made him want to tell the truth.

Velebit: It's not entirely my family's fault. We came to Aus as refugees after the Bosnian War. Google it sometime. Dad has PTSD and drinking makes it worse. This was the first Christmas away from his parents, but the long drive down to Sydney made it impossible, especially when he'd promised his staff they could have the afternoon off and he'd take the shift no one wanted. Because they always went to callouts in pairs, he had Leila on call, but he took one for the team by being in the office. If they got a call, he'd pick up Leila on the way to the job.

Crassostrea: Sorry to hear that. That sucks for him, and you. My dad was an immigrant too. He came here to go to uni ... so not the same thing at all.

Velebit: Nope. Mick's short response bounced into the gap between Crassostrea's messages. There was a huge difference between some bloke coming to Australia to swan around at university and arriving here with nothing but their clothes and a promise from a relative they'd never met. The cousin was technically his grandmother's cousin's grandkid, whose father had come to Aus after WWII. Regardless of the details of the relationship—still a cousin.

Crassostrea: From Thailand, so not the easiest road in the eighties. The White Aus Policy had just ended.

Perhaps not as easy as Mick had first assumed. Australia's history wasn't quite as ugly as Croatia's—a country forged from conflicts of all types including the Balkan Wars, both World Wars and the more recent Yugoslav wars—although that probably depended on perspective. Everything he'd read about what happened to the Aboriginal people sounded dreadful, and the White Australia policy was a stain on the country he'd grown up in.

Velebit: That sounds super tough.

Crassostrea: He didn't talk about it much.

Velebit: Past tense?

Crassostrea: Died in an accident about a decade ago.

Velebit: I'm sorry. Mick scratched the back of his neck. Was that why Crassostrea was online on Christmas Day? Mick hadn't expected to find another Aussie online this morning—shouldn't they all be opening presents and hanging out with family or friends? Or at work?

Crassostrea: Thanks.

Mick didn't wait to examine whether he should talk to a virtual stranger about his family, and just leaped in. Every Christmas he felt this urge to vent about his messy emotions. Crassostrea might just understand. *Velebit: The wars in the nineties were rough. My father was a shop owner in a small town. He fought when he could, but mostly he travelled to buy goods for us to sell. He heard rumours of the Serbs killing off Muslim Bosniaks and said the Croats would be next. He really hoped his mother would be alright looking after his father without him.*

Crassostrea: Holy shit.

Velebit: Google it. Or not, it's horrible. Anyway, my mother had a cousin who was in Sydney, and we got them to sponsor us to come here.

Crassostrea: I'm glad you are safe.

Mick started to type thanks when another message popped up.

Crassostrea: Even if all you do is try and cheat me out of platinum! ☺

The shift away from the serious topic was exactly what Mick needed. He played this game to avoid real life, not wallow in it. The irony was that his cheating ex-boyfriend Xavier had been the one to introduce him to SDH, but Mick brushed that thought away just like he did every time his brain betrayed him with thoughts of Xavier. What he really needed was to focus on the game strategy...

Velebit: Where is your xmas spirit?

Crassostrea: Same place yours is.

Velebit: Hiding?

Crassostrea: Talking to a stranger on the internet about personal stuff to avoid real life.

A laugh burst out of Mick, loud in his lounge room, and a rush of emotion clenched at his gut. Whoever said internet friendships weren't real didn't get it.

Velebit: What are you avoiding?

Crassostrea: Attending a party with my ex.

Velebit: Sounds awkward.

Crassostrea: Tons! And you?

Velebit: I usually work a shift on xmas Day. It's good overtime pay, and since it's just me and my parents ... Mick wasn't ready to finish that sentence. It was too much to explain why he'd left Sydney, too many tangled threads; between his father's occasional outbursts and the drama with Xavier—not that what happened was really Xavier's fault—but Mick had needed some space away from it all. Besides, the job here was a promotion and should be good for his career.

Crassostrea: You mentioned PTSD earlier. From the war?

Mick cocked his head to the side. *Velebit: Yes.*

Crassostrea: That's rough.

Velebit: It is. When I was a kid, I didn't understand that it wasn't my fault, but as an adult, I get it. It was why he'd trained as a paramedic, so he could help when his father had an episode. Maybe he should have taken a few days to go and visit his family, instead of taking on the worst shift of the holiday season—Christmas evening and night—when all the alcoholic nonsense began. No, his staff appreciated the gesture, and it was a good way to begin his time as the local area supervisor. His mentor back in Sydney had always said never to ask the staff to do what you wouldn't do yourself. Good advice.

Crassostrea: Being an adult is overrated.

Velebit: Says the guy hanging out on SDH on xmas day!

Crassostrea: That's me. Trying to re-do my teen years by playing games all day.

Velebit: Hey, settle down. Adults can play too. Mick's cheeks heated a little at the accidental euphemism.

Crassostrea: *coughs* Is that an unsubtle pick up line?

Velebit: Only if you want it to be.

Crassostrea: Well...

Mick held his breath.

Crassostrea: You did say SDH was a queer hang out space.

Velebit: I'm not sending you a dick pic. I'm too old for that nonsense.

Crassostrea: LOL. I'm too sensible for that. Although I like the leap from 'play' to 'dick pic'. Dude...

Velebit: I said I WOULDN'T send you one.

Crassostrea: You still went there. Shall we start somewhere less risqué?

Velebit: *swallows*

Velebit: Undo. I didn't mean it like that.

Crassostrea: *blushes* How did you mean it?

Velebit: Can we start again? Mick glanced down at the time. Still an hour to fill in until he needed to leave for work. He couldn't use that as an excuse to log off. Besides, he was having too much fun bantering with Crassostrea to leave now. It was more likely he'd get pulled into this discussion and end up being late for work. He'd better set an alarm.

Crassostrea: Nope. I'm screenshotting this for next time you want a bargain.

Velebit: Hey, isn't that blackmail?

Crassostrea: Not if you sell me some gold ingots.

Mick laughed at the change in subject. *Velebit: We could trade platinum for gold?*

Crassostrea: Now you are talking.

Chapter 3

Mick flopped on his couch after a long dramatic shift. He shouldn't assume the day shift would be easier than nights. He'd worked the night shift for the week between Christmas and New Year's. Every day in the hours between waking up and heading back to work, he'd chatted for a couple of hours with Crassostrea. Mostly about the game, a lot of strategy stuff, and they'd quickly realised that if they teamed up, they'd make more gains than they would working against each other. Mick had steered clear of anything else about his old life in Sydney. Every day, he'd learned new facts about Crassostrea: his username meant oysters in Latin and he was a trained aquaculturalist.

Today was Mick's first day shift for a while and he should be making himself something to eat, but all he wanted to do was log in and chat with Crassostrea. Besides, a pretty wild thing happened at work today and Mick wanted to share the story.

Velebit: How's things?

Crassostrea: I'm not sure.

That didn't sound good. Mick put his story about the day's adventure aside. *Velebit: Oh? Can I help?*

Crassostrea: Dunno.

Velebit: I'm a good listener.

Crassostrea: Yeah, I know. I do need to talk about this with someone, and my brother is a bit busy right now.

Mick frowned. He'd assumed Crassostrea lived alone; he knew he had an ex since he'd mentioned not wanting to go to a Christmas party with him, but had no other reason for his guess, except Mick lived alone too. *Velebit: Your brother?*

Crassostrea: We work together in the family business. He's older than me and usually good for a chat.

Velebit: But he's too busy?

Crassostrea: Not really his fault. Hey? Are you sure you want to hear this?

Velebit: We are friends, aren't we? It's what friends do.

When Crassostrea didn't reply, Mick kept typing rather than stop to think too much about what it might mean that Crassostrea hadn't responded to his mention of friendship. *Velebit: Plus. I had a wild day at work today and I could do with some distraction.*

Crassostrea: It must be a day for it.

Velebit: You ok?

Crassostrea: Yeah. Just a bit shaken.

Mick rubbed his temple. That didn't sound good at all. *Velebit: Oh?*

Crassostrea: I'm not even sure where to start.

Velebit: Anywhere you want. Mick added a gif of someone cupping their ear with 'I'm listening' written on the bottom.

Crassostrea: *breathes deep* I got handcuffed today.

Mick's lungs tightened. What on earth had happened today if the cops were involved? Must be a day for it—was it a full moon or something? *Velebit: Shit. You ok?*

Crassostrea: Maybe. *sighs* This might take a while to type, go and grab a coffee or something.

Mick added a gif of someone sipping a glass of wine, while he actually sipped his water. He didn't drink in the evenings when he was on the day shift, and not at all when he was on nights; pretty much didn't drink much anytime because he spent his working life dealing with the fallout when people drank too much. One beer on a weekend or a special occasion was enough for him.

Crassostrea: LOL. Ok, long story. Basically, our accountant has been stealing from our business.

Velebit: The one you run with your brother?

Mick's leg started to jiggle as the three little dots popped up to show Crassostrea was typing. Eventually a new message arrived.

Crassostrea: You've been listening! Yes. Anyway, my brother's missus, Zoe, figured it out and confronted him—the accountant, not my brother—and the accountant flipped out. He tried to kidnap her. Kiet, my bro, and I got a message from her and rushed into town in the ute to help. And then the wildest thing ... The accountant had planned to shoot Zoe at our farm, but she convinced him to stop on the edge of the road. Probably because his plan made no sense. WTF was he thinking? Anyway, we got there just as he pulled a gun on her, and Kiet tackled him. Zoe called the cops, and they arrested everyone until they figured out what happened. So fucking weird to get handcuffed after helping save my brother's missus from being shot.

Mick gulped as he read the message. It would be the most incredible coincidence for the same thing to happen in two different locations in Australia on the same day. How on earth could he tell Crassostrea that he'd been the paramedic who'd been on the scene? He'd treated Kiet's broken ribs and driven him into the local hospital. Oh hell, he'd checked Crassostrea for injuries. He'd touched him without knowing who he was. Crassostrea—oyster—oh my God, he was part of the Rainbow Cove Oyster Farm business. They literally lived down the road from each other.

Velebit: Wow. Are you ok? Mick knew Crassostrea was physically fine, he'd been the one to check him, but he hadn't stuck around to find out what happened next as he'd taken Kiet and Zoe into the hospital. Asking—again—if Crassostrea was okay was boring but it was all he could manage as he tried to process this revelation.

Crassostrea: I think so. The one positive is that we solved the mystery and we can get the business back on track now.

Mick had to say something now; a delay would make this more awkward. *Velebit: Confession time.*

Crassostrea: Sounds ominous.

Velebit: My name is Mick and I was the paramedic who treated your brother today.

Mick stared at his laptop, holding his breath. After what felt like ages, three dots appeared.

Crassostrea: Sam. And thank you.

Crassostrea: Also, WTF? We live in the same town?

Velebit: Apparently. I moved here a month ago. Mick had met Crassostrea online while he was still living in Sydney. Xavier had mentioned the game, and Mick had played it a bit, nothing serious, just to see what the fuss was about. And to keep an eye on Xavier. Mick huffed, ignoring the annoying twist in his stomach. Since moving to Marandowie, he'd become hooked—not just because of Crassostrea ... Sam—but also because he was a bit lonely as a newcomer to town with tricky working hours and there was always someone in the game to talk to, no matter when he was online.

Crassostrea: Why? What on earth motivated you to move to Marandowie?

Velebit: A job. I got offered a promotion to supervisor.

Crassostrea: Makes sense. Not many other reasons to move here.

Velebit: Isn't this a tourist hot spot?

Crassostrea: Apparently ... Nah, it is. Lots of people come here to visit the Rainbow Cove resort. It's the new Byron Bay, according to the marketing.

Velebit: So cynical.

*Crassostrea: *sighs* I shouldn't be. I love our farm. The cove is gorgeous, it's just that growing up in a small town is a bit claustrophobic. And wtf man ... You live here?*

*Velebit: *cackles* It's a surprise to me too. Wanna have coffee sometime?* Mick's cheeks warmed as he took a chance and asked Crassostrea ... Sam ... on a date. No, just coffee.

Crassostrea: Sure. Sounds good.

The casual response helped ease the butterflies in Mick's stomach a little.

Crassostrea: Give me a few days to finish sorting out this mess with the cops and then we can figure out a time that suits us both.

Velebit: Ok. I'm on days for the next three days, then it's my weekend ... let me check the schedules to find an afternoon sometime.

Crassostrea: That's a better time for beer. Pub dinner one evening?

Mick swallowed. A date in the local pub with locals watching on? *Velebit: Sounds like a plan. Hey, did Witch-Watcher take the bait and sell you the shipment of lava?* Switching back to game strategy would give Mick some time to process this incredible news. The man he'd been chatting to online lived in the same town he'd just moved to. He wracked his brain for an image, but the whole afternoon's events had been busy and most of his focus had been on the injured man. The man who'd turned out to be Sam's brother. And Mick had assumed the action would be the most dramatic thing to happen today. Not much could be more of an adrenaline rush than turning up to a fight scene with a gun in country Australia. Apparently he was wrong. Learning he lived in the same small town as his online friend, Crassostrea, made his head spin.

Chapter 4

Sam tugged at his collar again. It was two weeks since Velebit had mentioned having a beer together, and here he was in the local pub waiting for him. Paramedic schedules were a nuisance and it'd taken them ages to find an evening that worked for them both; well, for Velebit. Sam's farm work was always done by mid-afternoon each day. He breathed out. He'd already drunk half his beer, sipping nervously as he waited for Velebit. Mick. He checked his watch again. It wasn't even the agreed time yet—Sam was ridiculously early for their date. Date. Oh God, should he just leave? No. Don't panic. He'd already given himself way too much time to get here from the farm, and now had to waste time flicking through his phone and trying not to glance at the door of the pub constantly. Mick would turn up and he'd be, like, seventy or something. Or creepier in real life than he was online.

Damn it, why couldn't he remember anything about the paramedic who'd helped Kiet and Zoe? That whole day was a blur of emotion. It'd been a fortnight since then, and his heart still thumped quicker when he thought about how he'd pulled on the handbrake as Kiet had leaped from the ute and run into danger. Everything had moved too fast and simultaneously in slow motion, like he'd been holding his breath for too long under water and his lungs screamed for air as he tried to find the surface. The only thing that had mattered was ensuring Kiet would be fine. The grazes on his elbows had healed since then; minor grazes from wrestling Andersen on a gravel driveway.

As soon as Kiet was cleared from hospital with only a broken rib and plenty of bruises, Zoe had moved into the cottage, and now Sam knew how Kiet had felt when Lizzy had moved in. The cottage seemed much smaller with three of them living there, even though Zoe was amazing. She was the perfect match for Kiet. His grumpy brother had visibly relaxed with Zoe there, and it was so good to see him happy. Kiet had spent so many years trying to be everything for Sam: an older brother, a family, and the business manager trying to keep Rainbow Cove Oyster Farm afloat. He deserved every success and happiness, and Sam was so glad Zoe had arrived in their lives.

'Hello. Sam?' A rich voice infiltrated Sam's racing thoughts, and he glanced up to see a beautiful man standing beside his table. Medium height, short brown hair, broad shoulders under a neat collared shirt. Gosh, the man practically vibrated with masculine beauty in a slightly hardened way that appealed to Sam on more than an aesthetic level. If this man was Mick, how had he not noticed him that day? Sam half-stood, then sat again when Mick waved his hand.

'Yes, that's me. Mick?'

'Hi.' Mick slid into the seat opposite. He'd only spoken a few syllables, and yet each one was deliberate and precise with a timbre that slid over his skin in a delightful way.

'What do you want? I'll grab it.' Sam jumped out of his chair again.

'Just a beer. I'll have whatever you are having.'

'Okay. Cool. Cool. Cool.' Jeez, Sam, hold it together. He strode to the bar, his palms slightly clammy. His online buddy was freaking hot; broad-shouldered—had he thought that already?—with warm brown eyes in a lean face, and a hint of a dimple under his stubbled cheeks. Enough character in his face to make his stated thirty years seem accurate, yet young enough that he wasn't intimidating. Yeah, whatever. Mick was bloody sexy and that in itself was intimidating. The rush of attraction spread like a fever in Sam's veins, inching over his skin, and it took all his concentration to walk steadily to the bar without staring back over his shoulder.

Like, the last thing he needed right now was to trip over because he was staring at Mick instead of looking where he was going. He nodded at the barkeep, a pimply youth who was surely only barely the right age to serve him, ordered two beers and paid. He held them a bit too tightly as he strode back to the table where Mick sat nonchalantly.

'Thanks. I finished up nights this morning, and have tonight off, otherwise I'd be drinking a mocktail or something.' Mick sipped his beer and breathed out. 'That's excellent.'

'It's brewed locally. Well, a few towns up the coast, but that's kind of local, I guess.' *Stop rambling, Sam.*

'Good choice. Hey, thanks for coming. I wasn't sure if I should ask. It's a—'

'—weird situation.' They spoke in unison and Sam chuckled under his breath.

'It sure is. Thanks for helping my brother.'

Mick's cheeks coloured slightly. 'No problem. It's my job.'

'How long have you been an ambulance driver?'

'Paramedic,' Mick growled.

Sam frowned. 'Did I say something wrong?'

'We aren't drivers. We're paramedics. There's a big difference.'

'Sorry. What's the difference? If you don't mind me asking.' He scrambled to fix the conversation which he'd somehow screwed up.

'Driver is old-fashioned and undermines the amount of qualifications needed to be a paramedic.'

Sam nodded. 'I get it. It's kind of like someone saying I'm just a farmer when I have a Masters in aquaculture.'

'Something like that. The amount of training needed to be a paramedic is huge and saying "driver" makes it sound like we just jump in the van and race around without the skills needed to save lives.' Mick crossed his arms over his chest and Sam tried not to notice the way his pecs bulged. He swallowed.

'Makes sense.' He dragged in a deep breath. 'Can we start again? Without my misstep.'

Mick grinned, one side of his mouth kicking up higher than the other. 'Sure.' Damn him for looking so gorgeous.

'How long have you been a paramedic?' Sam held his breath until Mick's smile grew wider.

'All of my career. It's the only thing I ever wanted to do. I mean, I get to save people's lives, and every day is different. Plus I get to drive very fast.' Mick winked and Sam let out the breath he'd been holding.

'So driving is a bonus, but not the core of the job.' Sam wrapped his hand tighter around his glass.

Mick laughed. 'Basically, yes. You'll offend every paramedic if you call them just a driver, but we all love speed!'

'Do you have to do much training for that?'

'Yes.' Mick's short answer made Sam feel a bit foolish—of course they needed training to drive fast, like, imagine if they crashed or something. That'd hardly be helpful to anyone. After a pause, it was obvious Mick wasn't going to add anything further. Sam gulped down the rest of the beer he'd been nursing before Mick's arrival. He'd need to get a ride home at this rate and he mentally calculated when Zoe would finish work. He could text her for a lift, then collect his ute tomorrow.

'So you've been here in Marandowie your whole life?' Mick asked.

Sam tried not to grimace at the suggestion he was a small-town boy; it was his own doubt that created that assumption, not Mick's or anyone else's. 'Pretty much. Like, I went away to Sydney for some of school and uni, but then came back to help my brother run the farm.'

'I grew up in Cabramatta, you know, western Sydney. It's a suburb with lots of immigrants, like my family, so it wasn't too brutal growing up there as a newcomer to Australia. My Croatian accent disappeared quite fast though.'

Mick looked around the pub, and Sam tried to see his local from an outsider's point of view. For a small town in Australia, Marandowie had a fairly diverse population. The growing tourist market and the excellent farming land brought in plenty of trade from everywhere; it was a nice place for immigrant families to get a good start at a new life. Sam's papa had come here in the eighties to go to university and had worked a summer holiday job on the oyster farm owned and run by his mum. Papa had fallen in love and never left, never finishing the degree he'd come to do, which was partly why Sam was so determined to get his own qualifications. His parents had died in an accident when he was sixteen, and his Masters was his way of remembering them. Of honouring the work Mum and Papa had done at the farm to give them all a better life.

'Marandowie and Rainbow Cove aren't as diverse as Sydney, but it's not the mostly white enclave that you get in some small towns.' Sam had a friend at uni, Derek, who'd been the only Asian in his small town, and Sam was glad that there were several Asian families at Marandowie High. He and his siblings, Nok and Kiet, were the only ones with a Thai father; the other families were of Chinese and Vietnamese descent.

'True. My staff here are a good mix. I was happily surprised, especially after working in Sydney with a diverse range of people. It's always a risk moving to a new place when...' Mick leaned forward and whispered, 'gay.'

'You can say it at a normal volume. You aren't the only queer person in town, and this place has changed since I was at school. I went to school with Zoe—you met her when our accountant tried to shoot her. Anyway, we were in the same class, and I still remember the drama and gossip that flew around the town when her sister Jade came out. Like, Zoe and Jade's parents are super religious, so they were basically the worst.'

'That sucks so much. I hate that bigotry splits up families like that.'

Sam shrugged. 'Their loss. Zoe is a wonderful person. I don't know her sister very well, but my point was that most of the town were supportive to Jade. Rainbow Cove used to be a bit hippie when I was a kid, and it was great to see so many people offer their homes to Jade and Zoe when their parents kicked them out.'

Mick blinked and smiled a little. 'That's great. Are you saying I should just be me and not worry about getting beaten up?'

Sam rolled his eyes. 'Every town has their shitty elements. I'd steer clear of David Smythe and his crowd. And I probably wouldn't stand up in the pub and declare that you're intending to have amazing gay sex with me.' He hadn't meant to blurt that—damn Mick for being so bloody handsome—and his cheeks screamed with heat.

'I am?' Mick raised one eyebrow and the look he sent Sam only increased the glow on his face.

Sam picked up his beer and sipped some without breaking eye contact with Mick. Hopefully flirty, but also trying to hide a little. 'Maybe not on the first date. I mean, like, I don't really have a no sex on the first date policy or anything. Oh God. Can you stop looking at me like that?'

'Like I want to drag you behind the pub and bang you?'

Sam gulped and nearly choked on his beer. He spluttered and shook his head. 'You do? But we've only just met.'

Mick tilted his head slightly to the left. 'We met months ago.'

'IRL, I meant,' pronouncing the acronym as one word rather than spelling out the letters.

'We can go slow if that's what you need.'

Sam closed his eyes for a long second and tried to calm his pulse. 'Slow is a good plan. I've just come through a break-up. I don't think rebound sex is a good idea.' He'd always wonder if he was just moving from one relationship to another, and after everything Lizzy had said, Sam knew he needed to take some time to be single and well ... grow up. She'd been right on that front, not that he wanted to admit it aloud to anyone. Kiet had stepped up when their parents had died and had sheltered Sam from needing to grow up too fast. Did that mean he hadn't grown up at all? He was so confused about it. And what did growing up mean anyway? He wasn't going to give up playing Sky Disc Hooks just because of someone else's notion that gaming was only for kids. Screw that.

'Rebound sex?'

Sam needed to stop digging this damned hole. He forced himself to look at Mick, to stare at those gorgeous features and get out of his own head. 'I'm making a mess of this, aren't I?'

'A little. It's cute.' Mick's eyes danced with laughter, all crinkled at the edges, and Sam's fingertips twitched with a sudden need to touch him.

'Cute? Yeah, that's totally the vibe I was going for.' Better than looking like a messy disaster. He ran his hand through his hair. Why hadn't he gotten a haircut for today? OMG, he'd be more bloody anxious if he'd gone to the trouble of doing that.

'By the way, doing that with your hair only makes you cuter.' Mick reached up and flicked a lock of hair off Sam's forehead. Mick's touch sent a jolt of energy across his skin, and the air seemed to crackle between them even after Mick leaned back in his chair and crossed his arms again. Sam couldn't form any words, just gaped at Mick and his amazing pecs and biceps, drawn into his hungry stare.

'Want to order some food?' Sam cringed at the slight squeak in his voice. The stare Mick gave him wasn't that type of hungry, but damn, Sam needed to do something, because at this rate, he was on the verge of making an impulsive choice. One he might regret.

'Sure.' How could Mick sound so casual?

Sam's whole body felt alight and his heart raced. 'I'll grab some menus.' Perhaps a few quick strides to the bar would calm everything down. Thankfully he'd worn jeans, so his erection shouldn't be too noticeable. Hopefully. This was all a lot easier when they were Velebit and Crassostrea chatting online about geeky things. Part of Sam wanted to go back to the time when he didn't know how sexy Velebit was, when everything was much less confusing and complicated. One thing was true—he couldn't leap from one relationship into another. Lizzy had made some good points and he needed to spend the time on himself before he committed to someone else. It was a shame, because Mick was right here in town, looking like that with the added benefit of sharing the same passion for SDH as him. A geek and a friend, with a smoking body.

Sam was in so much trouble.

Chapter 5

Mick stared at Sam's ass—very fine indeed—as he rushed off to the bar to grab some menus and tried his best not to think about the glimpse he'd seen of Sam's erection pressed against his jeans as he stood up. How had they ended up here? Chatting about sex as if it was a real possibility. Sam was right though—he couldn't leap into a relationship so soon after moving here; it wasn't wise. Ahh, when had he ever been wise? He hadn't been lying when he told Sam he was cute. He was the same geeky person he was online, with an added amount of funny awkwardness, as if he wasn't sure how to deal with seeing Mick in real life. IRL, as Sam had said, pronouncing it like 'earl' which was totally adorable. Floppy black hair and brown eyes that glowed with intelligence and humour, combined with a lean body that reflected Sam's life as a farmer. Under his neat collared shirt and jeans, Mick would bet that Sam was perfectly sculpted with muscles crafted through work. He couldn't come onto him too strongly, not when Sam had showed reticence after their eye-opening discussion on sex. When he'd agreed to meet Sam, two weeks ago, he hadn't expected a mutual instant attraction. The last two weeks had been filled with work and life—the usual holiday busy period meant more paperwork than usual too—and he'd barely given this outing a second thought. Was the attraction he felt mutual? Mick didn't think he'd imagined the heat between them, or the way Sam's eyes had widened when Mick had crossed his arms and deliberately flexed his pecs a little. Or the tell-tale erection pressing against his jeans. The 'is he gay or not' dance didn't need to happen, since they'd discussed it online, but just being gay and single and in the same town didn't necessarily translate into more. Mick had met plenty of queer men in Sydney who he had no physical interest in, and finding someone cute who also fascinated him was even rarer. Maybe it was time he settled down. No, he'd tried that once before and it'd been a complete disaster.

Sam passed him a menu and he tried not to breathe a sigh of relief at having something to do that wasn't self-examination.

'What's good here?' Mick asked.

'Shahid is the chef here and his curries are legendary. He was born here in Aus—' That Sam had to deliberately make this point made Mick wonder about how people in the town saw Sam. Mick didn't have to try too hard to understand; he occasionally got mistaken for being Middle Eastern or Lebanese, which came with its own brand of underhanded rubbish, but mostly he was seen as white and no one questioned where he was born or if he should be here. '—His parents are from Bangaluru, and he really brings authentic southern Indian flavours into his cooking. His parma is pretty special too, if you like a dash of heat in the tomato sauce. Shahid makes it himself.' Sam paused for a second. 'You probably know Shahid's wife, Keerthi; she works for the ambulance, I think.'

Mick nodded. 'I do know her. Keerthi is a very skilled paramedic. Brilliant, really. This region is so lucky to have her. Honestly, she probably should have been given my job. She's qualified for it and she knows the region better than me. It's a tough situation for her.'

Sam didn't respond, just read the menu for a while, and Mick succumbed to the urge to explain more.

'Being a man, and a white immigrant, even growing up in Cabramatta, hasn't equipped me with the skills to figure out how to solve this.' Mick had stepped into an unfair situation and had no clue about how to fix it. Had Keerthi missed out on the job because she was a woman, or because she had a foreign-sounding name and everything that went with that? He'd met the state boss who approved Mick's employment and he'd come across as the type of bloke who wouldn't employ a young woman in a supervisor role because she might get pregnant. It was enraging; throw in the potential for racism as well as sexism and the whole situation sucked. He had exactly the same qualifications as Keerthi, although maybe—hopefully—his experience working in Sydney was the difference between them as candidates for the job. On paper, she had local knowledge while he brought in the skills gained working in a busier environment. In his opinion, the job could have gone to either of them.

'"Solve" is an interesting choice of a word.' Sam glanced up. 'The first thing you need to do is listen to Keerthi and see what she wants. It's good that you see the problem and want to do something, but she doesn't need a saviour who doesn't listen to her needs.'

'Okay. That's really helpful.' Mick paused to let Sam's opinion sink in properly. 'Thanks. I appreciate your view on this one. I feel a bit clueless about this stuff.'

'I might have the parma. You?' Sam changed the subject and Mick knew he needed to let it go. It wasn't fair to ask Sam for more advice about Keerthi and potential systematic sexism and racism; not when he had the internet.

'Since you recommend Shahid's cooking, I'll have the chicken tikka masala. Let me get this.'

Mick paused. 'You got the beers, let this be my shout.'

Sam nodded. 'Thanks.'

Ordering their meals helped give Mick a little space from the intense conversation. Perhaps he shouldn't have talked about his work problems on a first date; it was a bit too much to throw a complicated problem into what should be a light conversation. That was the problem with already having formed a relationship online: he knew an odd collection of information about Sam and was sorely lacking in other areas. Once everything was ordered and paid for, he slid back into his seat and put the buzzer on the table.

'What do people do around here for fun?' Mick asked, purely to discover what Sam liked to do for fun. He didn't particularly care what other locals got up to, and besides, he'd already been to enough car accidents and pub brawls since he'd moved here to have a fair clue about what some of them did.

'Lots of people play sport, plus we have the cove and the ocean beach, so fishing, surfing, stuff like that. There's a CWA, and the library runs a few book clubs. A couple of people I went to school with are in a band. The usual stuff.'

'Okay, what about you? What do you do when you aren't working?'

Sam wrinkled up his nose and shrugged. 'SDH.'

'And?' Mick fished for more information. Surely Sam didn't just work, then hang out on the internet?

'Hey, I'm not some loser who just works and plays internet games.'

Mick raised both eyebrows. 'Who said the word "loser"? I play the same game. No judgement here.'

'Sure.' Sam grinned. 'It's a bit dorky, but I dive and do underwater photography.'

'That's cool. Why would you think it's dorky?'

Sam shook his head, still smiling. 'Because it's still basically work. I dive at our farm and take the photos to catalogue what's living around our farm. Knowing the different species helps me understand the seasons and the health of the farm.'

'Whenever you say "farm", I imagine grass and paddocks, not water.'

Sam rolled his eyes. 'City boy. I'll take you out on the boat sometime and you can have a look for yourself. Actually, no, the resort has just partnered with us to do kayak tours of the farm. You should do one of those. The first one is next week.'

Mick's breath stuck in his throat. 'I'd rather *you* showed me.' The blush on Sam's face was worth the flirty comment, and even though they'd agreed to go slowly, Mick couldn't help it.

'Sure. I think the tour is booked out anyway.'

'Are you unwilling to spend more time with me?' Mick hated how the question came out all needy. They'd connected so easily online, with none of this hesitation, and he wondered if Sam was slowly changing his mind about him. This was why Mick didn't date. It'd been easier in Sydney: just go to a club, hook up with someone, have safe sex, and go home alone. He was lying to himself, thinking that one of the reasons he'd taken this job was because he was bored with that life. The truth was he needed to get away and have a fresh start. Somewhere he wouldn't keep running into Xavier's friends.

'It's not that. There is this—' Sam waved his hands awkwardly '—between us and I think it's sensible not to rush in just yet.'

Mick wanted to tease and tell Sam not to be sensible. He certainly felt the potential heat between them too, a chemistry in the air that made sensual promises, and was far too tempting. 'Okay. You really do want to go slowly?' He needed to be certain because he really wanted to push past all the boundaries between them and beg Sam to relax. As if that would work.

'I have some stuff to work out.' Sam looked like he was trying not to grimace—either that or he had a gut cramp.

'It's you, not me?' Mick glanced at the buzzer, urging it to vibrate and save him from this sudden influx of awkwardness.

'I know it's a cliché. Look, I like you.' Sam's tongue darted out and licked his bottom lip, almost distracting Mick from the rush of blood to his head at Sam's confession. He liked him. The comment sent a giddy wave through Mick's brain. 'We are friends, and when I agreed to meet you, I didn't expect ... Well—' Sam made the awkward gesture again, a circle of his hand vaguely in the direction of Mick's body.

Mick wanted to roll his shoulders to ease the growing tension. 'I understand.' He wasn't sure he did. It would probably increase the tension in the air if he asked for clarification—did Sam mean that he thought Mick was hot and that was confusing? Because that's how Mick felt about Sam. He wasn't sure what he'd expected exactly from Crassostrea's profile. He'd come here on the hope that he would enjoy having a beer with a mate, a mate with no connection to his old life. This growing roar of desire made the whole dinner complicated, not to mention the potential for the future. Mick had the sense that he needed to say exactly the right thing, or he'd mess up his chance at getting to know Sam better—in bed or out.

'Thank you. I just don't want to rush this and then regret it because I have a tendency to leap head first into things without thinking it through.' The frown on Sam's face deepened. 'Be assured, if I *didn't* like you, I'd be up for a quickie, soooo...' Mick dragged out the last word and rubbed his forehead.

'Thank you.'

Mick wanted to add that he'd done that too many times and it wasn't as satisfying as it ought to be. A bed partner who was hot but not that likeable was a temporary high that didn't last. Instead, he said, 'I also like you. You are genuinely the same as you are online, which is a pleasant thing.' Mick's stilted attempt to ease the tension between them and reassure Sam—or was it himself?—was interrupted by a loud buzz. Their food was ready. He breathed out quickly and audibly. 'Wait here.' He jumped and rushed off to the counter to pick up their plates. After he placed them on the table, Sam reached out and tapped his fingers across Mick's wrist. Mick's skin zinged and he dragged his hand away. Not because Sam's touch repulsed him: the complete opposite.

'Hey. Maybe one day we'll look back on this and laugh at the weirdness.'

'Or we'll move on and it'll be nothing much.'

Sam scoffed. 'Now that's depressing.'

'Yeah. Why is it so much easier to talk through a keyboard?' Mick picked up his utensils and scooped up a forkful of rice and chicken tikka masala. The taste exploded in his mouth. 'OMG, you were right. This is incredible.'

'Shahid is a genius. We are lucky to have him in Marandowie.' Sam cut into his schnitzel; the melted cheese on top oozed under the tomato sauce covering the parma.

'That looks great too.'

Sam glanced up from his plate. 'The key to a good parma is the right sauce, gooey cheese, but most importantly, a schnitzel that's still thick and juicy. The sauce shouldn't be used to compensate for dry meat.'

'You've given this a lot of thought.'

Sam grinned. 'Or I've eaten a lot of pub meals. I think I existed on ramen and chicken parma while I was at uni.'

'Those are pretty balanced meals. Ergh, I didn't mean to sound so old.' Mick tucked into his own meal so he wouldn't have to see Sam's reaction. The sound of Sam's laughter rumbled around him, and he risked a glance up.

'I mean, you are so much older than me,' Sam said. If Mick hadn't been looking he wouldn't have seen the way Sam winced.

'Are you alright?'

Sam laid down his cutlery. 'My ex thought I needed to grow up, that's why we broke up. It's a bit of a sore point.'

'Right. I'll keep all comments about my lengthy life experience to myself then. Look, I don't see why someone might say that about you. Perhaps it's as simple as them not understanding the gaming world.'

'Because only teens and losers play games?' Sam held up his hands. 'Just so you know, I don't think that. It was sarcasm, you know, like, but maybe that's what they meant. I don't know. I need to figure it out for myself.'

'Take your time.'

'Because I'm just a baby and I've got lots of it?'

Mick's head jerked up. 'No. I didn't mean that.'

'It's okay.' Sam's mouth twisted ruefully. 'I was joking, mostly.'

'Your ex really did a number on you. I'm sorry.' Mick knew exactly how that felt, and a nagging pain twinged his gut as he pushed away his past. Why did chatting to Sam make all these nasty memories resurface?

Sam wriggled in his seat. 'Don't be sorry. I'm the one who stayed for too long in a relationship that was on the rocks. I should've been brave enough to end it. Staying was convenient and that's not the best choice I could have made.' He scratched the back of his neck.

Mick wished he could do more to reassure Sam. 'I get it. I've made plenty of mistakes in my time. Staying too long in a relationship because it's easier to stay than confronting the truth is easy to do. Don't blame yourself too much.' If only he could take his own advice ... and not blame himself for not listening whenever Xavier said he wanted to leave. The factory fire had been the catalyst for them finally breaking up, but Xavier had left and come back many times before then. Mick blamed himself for not being enough for Xavier.

'Thanks. It's more complicated than that, but yeah, thanks.'

Mick held his cutlery a little tighter to stop him reaching out for Sam's hand. 'Life is pretty damned complicated. Look at us.'

'Yeah.'

They ate in silence after that, with the sounds of the pub all around, leaving Mick to wonder what Sam had meant by that single 'yeah'. Yeah, he agreed with him? Yeah, this was too complicated, and he'd never see him again? Or yeah, give it time and there was hope for something more? After the final mouthful of his excellent meal, he wiped his mouth with a napkin.

'Thanks for meeting me. It's been great.'

Sam glanced up with his eyebrows slightly raised. 'Great? It's been socially awkward and way too revealing.'

'Are you always this honest?'

'What other options are there? I'm just a simple oyster farmer, Mick.'

Mick smiled. 'Most people would say a social white lie and agree. They'd said, "yeah, great to meet you" and say something like, "I'll call you" and that'd be it.'

A frown flashed over Sam's face for a second. 'I won't need to call. I'll see you online.'

'Probably later tonight.' They both chuckled and Mick knew this wouldn't be the last time he'd see Sam.

'Same time next week, then?' Mick asked. He mentally ran over his schedule and he was pretty sure he was free.

'Sure.' Sam stood up and held out his hand, so Mick stood too and shook it. A jolt of energy flowed up his arm, tingling in his chest, and as he watched Sam walk out of the pub, he clenched his fist a couple of times. Eventually he gave his hand a shake because the buzz on his skin just wouldn't go away.

Chapter 6

Sometimes Sam wished he was more impulsive, and that everyone else's thoughts about how he should behave didn't get into his head and disrupt what he really wanted. It would be easy to blame his past relationships on neediness—his older sister Nok had disappeared when he was just a small boy, and then his parents died when he was sixteen. Basic psychology might say he was trying to hold onto people too tightly, so they wouldn't leave too, and that's why Lizzy found him stifling. Except that didn't sit quite right with him: it was too straightforward, and he hated the idea that he was boringly obvious.

The dinner with Mick had been far too awkward—to the point where he'd spent days reliving every piece of the discussion and had avoided going online to play SDH in case Mick was online too. But enough was enough. He couldn't just stop doing the things he liked; he missed the strategy of the game and he had other friends and cousins on there that he wanted to catch up with. Being hamstrung by social awkwardness wasn't how he wanted to live his life, except that whenever he sat down to log in, the image of Mick filled his brain. So hot, so comfortable in his own skin, and with more life experience and ... everything. Mick was just a bit too much, too perfectly attractive, for Sam. And older, which shouldn't matter, but it did. Like, he really needed to get past this hang-up.

He logged on and clicked onto his DMs. There were about six messages from Velebit. He read through the messages, mostly about the game, but the last one made Sam smile.

Velebit: Were you serious when you said you'd show me your farm?

Sam couldn't resist, especially because Velebit was currently online too. *Crassostrea: Is that a euphemism?*

Velebit: Ha, no. It's a nice day and I haven't seen you for a few days.

*Crassostrea: *blushes* Do you miss me?*

Velebit: A little. You haven't been online.

Crassostrea: I've been busy, besides you've already seen me once. Sam wanted to brush away Mick's keenness to see him again as simple curiosity, but even he couldn't forget the crackle of chemistry between them. He wanted to see Mick again too, to find out if it was just a fluke, or something more.

Velebit: Twice.

Crassostrea: The first one doesn't count. I didn't know who you were.

Velebit: True. My memory of you that day is vague too.

Sam grinned, glad it wasn't just him.
Crassostrea: Come on then, invite yourself over.

Velebit: Today?

Sam glanced at the time on his computer. He'd just finished the morning shift and soon Kiet would come up from the shed for lunch.
Crassostrea: Sure. I need to do a few checks this afternoon, but you can join me.

Velebit: I'll be there shortly.

Crassostrea: So keen!

Velebit added a gif of Brick Man from Lego Masters saying 'I'm so pumped'. Sam didn't bother to hide his smile as he shut down SDH, and as the backdrop photo popped up on his screen, he realised SDH was their only means of communication. He probably should grab Mick's mobile number. Maybe later when he turned up at the farm, or was that too soon?

***

Mick walked around the porch to see Sam in an old wooden chair, his legs outstretched with his ankles crossed. 'Come and sit. There's some iced water in that jar if you want a glass.'

Mick grabbed a clean glass and poured himself some water, then settled in an empty chair. After he sat down, he looked up and the view literally took his breath away. 'Wow.'

'Huh?'

'The view. It's something else.'

Sam smiled, a slow, almost seductive grin that stopped Mick's breath—again—as if both Sam and the view over the water held his lungs hostage.

'We are very lucky. I mean, the farm is hard work, and this cottage is falling down around us, but every day Kiet and I get to go to work right there.'

'I can definitely see the appeal. It would make the best country retreat.'

Sam snorted. 'Apart from the fact that our cottage is falling down?'

'Yeah, apart from that minor practicality.' Mick waved his arm in the direction of the water. 'Still, imagine how much people would pay to come here, stay in a cottage overlooking the bay.'

'They already do that at the resort.'

Mick nodded. 'Right, of course. The resort probably takes up all the tourist money for the area.'

'Since when have you had an interest in tourism?' Sam's rude framing of the question caused a bubble of laughter to stick in the back of Mick's throat. Since moving here and taking on the new challenge of running a country town station, his old dream of running a small hotel or the like had begun to sneak back into his thoughts. He loved people and wanted to make them happy. For a long time, being a paramedic had let him help people, but it missed the element of making them smile. People didn't tend to smile when they were hurt and their lives were at a point of crisis.

'Oh, Sam. There is so much you don't know about me.'

'What does that mean?' Sam shifted in his chair and frowned at Mick.

'I'm teasing.' He wasn't ready to share that dream with anyone just yet, not when he didn't have any clarity himself.

'Okay?' Sam's frown slowly dissipated. 'Okay. Sure. Tease away.'

Mick chuckled. 'I'm serious though. I took this promotion because my life in Sydney wasn't—' he wasn't ready to talk about Xavier '—satisfying, and I hoped running my own station would be a good challenge.'

'And?'

'It is.'

'Why do I hear a "but" in that pause?'

Mick shrugged, trying to make the movement as casual as possible. 'The whole Christmas/New Year's period brings out the worst in people.

This week has made me realise that I'm tired of helping people who don't want to be helped.'

Sam's frown deepened and he raised one eyebrow. 'Pretty sure anyone who rings triple zero wants to be helped. Otherwise why call?'

'Look, most of the work we do is fulfilling and it does help people, but I also see a lot of the ugly parts of life and people. Repeat customers, like people beaten by their partners, but who don't leave.'

'I've read that leaving is often the most dangerous time.' Sam's sympathetic tone reminded Mick he was being unfair. It wasn't up to him to judge those in crisis.

Mick sighed. 'It is, and I've seen that it's not an easy decision. I guess I just don't understand the people who stay, who continue to forgive their abusers over and over. The ones who have an opportunity to leave but refuse to take it.' He shouldn't have begun this line of thinking; his eyes started to burn. He'd been that guy for too long, forgiving Xavier every time he decided he needed a regular boyfriend again. Like an ex-smoker, Mick both understood the craving for it, but also judged those who wouldn't quit much harder than he should. Besides, he'd hardly call his on–off relationship with Xavier abusive. They hadn't hit each other. Xavier had occasionally been a bit rough in bed, but that wasn't abuse, just a misunderstanding. Xavier was always sorry afterwards.

'Abuse isn't always obvious, and aren't the people who can't see that the very ones who need the most help?'

Mick gripped the chair tighter, so he didn't sway as all his blood fell to his feet. Sam didn't know about Xavier; he couldn't possibly know.

'I think my attitude is a symptom of burnout.' Mick pushed away the fragment of doubt that tried to scream at him about Xavier's unfairness and focused on other people. He'd had never had an issue with any of the rougher parts of his job, until now. What happened in Sydney after the factory fire was complicated by bad timing. Xavier had left to help his sister while Mick was recovering from his injuries. It wasn't Xavier's fault that his sister needed him, and he couldn't pay the rent. Mick couldn't afford their place on his own while on medical leave. Thankfully Mick's parents had welcomed him home and nursed him while he healed. Once he was better, the job was all he had left. He applied for this promotion to get out of town and away from all the confusing feelings. This week's domestic incidents had been sad for those people, but nothing to do with his own past. It was the lurch between work and having a wonderful dinner with Sam that created this sense of unease. He just wanted to sit here on Sam's porch and stare at the view, with Sam beside him. It was so peaceful, he hungered for it more than he ought from only one meeting IRL.

'Burnout is a serious matter. Not one that can be fixed by imagining running a bread and breakfast in a crappy little cottage out of a small town.'

'You're right. It's just the beauty of the view getting to me. Maybe all I need is a porch like this to sit on every day, overlooking the water, to help me refresh from a day of helping people.'

Sam laughed, a loud bark that rang out clear over the grass and water in front of them. 'Well, you could just keep inviting yourself over.'

Mick choked. The sly look on Sam's face as he raised one eyebrow, and the cheeky glint in his eyes, did nothing to slow the build-up of sexual tension in Mick's body. Damn.

'Want to come for a snorkel?' Sam bounced to his feet and held out his hand for Mick. He placed his hand in Sam's and pulled himself up. 'Oh. I meant for you to give your empty glass, not...'

'Not hold your hand, like we are a couple.'

'We aren't a couple.' But Sam didn't take his hand away and Mick made himself relax his grip, so he would know if Sam wanted to keep holding his hand.

'Not yet, but I know your online persona, and—' Mick leaned closer to Sam '—I adore the way you smell.' He didn't mean to blurt that out, but thinking about life back in Sydney had really done a number of him.

Sam wavered on his feet. 'You what?'

Mick had only one option: roll with it as if it was on purpose—plus it was true, so not really a hardship to mention. 'You smell so lovely, like lemon myrtle and sea salt and a little bit of something that can only be you.'

'Um, okay? Thanks.' A few pinpoints of red on Sam's cheeks made Mick wonder if he'd gone too far, too soon. That's what Xavier used to say sometimes. No. He wasn't going to ruin today with thoughts of his ex-boyfriend. What was up with that?

'It's not as creepy as it sounds.'

'Really? Cos it's a bit odd to think of you walking around sniffing at me.' The edges of Sam's brown eyes crinkled, and his mouth smirked as if he was holding back a laugh. The very image of himself following Sam like a puppy with his nose outstretched made Mick laugh, hard and loud. Awkward.

'That would be weird. I'm sorry, it's been a rough week and I wanted to come here and spend some time with you. And you...' He gritted his teeth to stop the rambling nonsense that seemed to keep falling out of his mouth.

'I what?' Sam hadn't moved away; if anything he'd leaned even closer to Mick. And he was still holding Mick's hand. Mick's skin tingled, gradually waking up to the growing desire between them. Sam's hands were callused and firm, and it took a few breaths before Mick knew what he needed to say.

'You welcomed me here like it was no big deal, like we've been friends for ages, not met once.'

'We have been friends for ages.' Sam touched his thumb to Mick's bottom lip.

Mick closed his eyes, unable to think with Sam's finger stroking his mouth like that.

'You really do smell great.' Mick breathed in deep to try and draw the salty lemon scent from Sam's skin into his lungs. Heat from Sam's gentle movements flowed into Mick's veins until everything buzzed pleasantly, and his jeans were too tight. He opened his eyes and gazed deep into Sam's eyes; their rich brown colour glistened in the sunlight. Mick was captivated by Sam, by his intelligent humour, his care, and the way his touch made Mick feel properly alive. He could imagine a life with him, one where they encouraged each other to be the best of themselves, where he could spend his evenings sitting on the deck with Sam, holding hands and watching the sunset together. Mick was caught up in the romanticism of the moment, as if he'd been given a view of the future and it was everything he'd ever wanted.

'It's my soap. Like, oyster farming isn't the nicest-smelling job, and there's a lady who lives in town who makes this amazing soap that cuts through the stench of it.'

Mick kissed Sam's fingers, and the only thing he could taste was salt and Sam. 'I can't taste anything.' Or rather, he couldn't taste the pungent stench Sam referred to, only the essence of Sam, which gave Mick too many ideas about the future he wanted.

'The soap?'

'No, the oyster thing.'

'Good. I'd hate to think my breath smelled like old oysters left too long in the sun. Gross.'

Mick licked his bottom lip, 'No. Nothing like that. You taste good.'

Sam laughed and stepped away, taking his fingers with him and leaving Mick wanting more. It felt good, not desperate and needy. He shook his head to clear away the remnant of his old life. Why did Xavier keep intruding now?

'Come on, time for snorkelling. Did you bring something to swim in?'

It took a moment for Mick's brain to kick in again. He clenched his hand, now empty and cold as Sam turned to face the view. 'Yes. After you teased me about thinking farms were all grass, I remembered to bring shorts.' He'd also brought a rash vest to cover his scarred back and shoulder.

'Okay. Give me that glass. You can get changed inside, and I'll see you down at the shed.' Sam waved in the direction of the large shed at the bottom of the hill, then disappeared back into the house. The way he teased him, and then stepped back into friendship, could have given Mick whiplash if he didn't already know Sam was fighting the same attraction he was. Sam wanted to take this slowly for his own reasons, and Mick loved that Sam found it hard to stick to his ideals on this one. The chemistry between them had only one outcome, and the anticipation of when they would finally end up in bed together added to the spark between them. They'd both get what they wanted ... in time. Mick stretched out his neck and shoulders. The wait was necessary, and it would be worth it.

Chapter 7

Sam always felt at home in the water. He pulled his shirt off over his head and left it on the seat of the boat, before slipping over the side and into the refreshing water of the river. The farm was located in the tidal zone of the river mouth, far enough up the river to have full coverage of the oysters all the time, but with enough of the tidal flow to make the water salty and bring in new nutrients twice a day. The water surrounded him, cool against his skin, and washed away the patina of sweat caused by the sticky heat of the day. He swam away from the boat, then back again and pulled himself up to peer over the side at Mick.

'Come in. It's gorgeous.'

'Okay?'

'It's fine. We hardly ever get sharks in here, and the boat is safely tied to the farm.' With the engine turned off, the farm was enveloped in a calm silence. Sam loved it here in the water, with his work beside him. He grinned, largely at himself; even his hobby involved spending time out here, taking photos of the life around the farm. That, and Sky Disc Hooks.

Mick stared over the side, his face slightly pale under his tan. 'Hardly ever?'

'I'm kidding. Come on, the water is beautiful today.' Sam had already taken the samples he needed for testing and had given Mick a bit of a tour of the farm as he'd gone about his job. The boat rocked as Mick jumped away from Sam, and a large splash sprayed over the boat, flicking droplets onto Sam's already wet face. He let go of the boat, and dove underneath it, swimming towards Mick's flailing legs. As tempting as it was to grab him by the ankle, Sam couldn't pull that trick on someone who wasn't familiar with the farm, especially not after his ill-advised shark joke. If it'd been Kiet, absolutely—they'd grown up swimming off the boat while their parents worked—but he couldn't freak out Mick like that. Instead he surfaced next to him. Mick wore a skin-tight short-sleeved dark-blue rash vest and matching board shorts.

'Told ya, it's lovely in the water.'

'It is. It would be better if I could touch the ground.'

Sam shook his head. 'You should've told me you can't swim.'

'I can swim. I'm just used to—' Mick drew in a deep breath, his nostrils flaring '—more controlled environments.'

'Oh, like swimming pools, where there are no creatures?'

'Yeah. And your shark comment—'

Sam chuckled. 'I shouldn't find that so funny. Here.' He reached out for the boat and grabbed a snorkel mask. 'Put this on. Take a look. You'd have to be lucky, or unlucky, to spot a shark.' After watching Mick try to tread water and fiddle with the snorkel for half a minute, Sam took pity on him and helped him out. 'Hold the rope with one hand, and I'll put the mask on you.'

'You planned this, didn't you?'

Sam grinned. 'Planned what?'

'Getting me into your territory so you could show off your skills.' Was it Sam's imagination, or did Mick rake his gaze over Sam's body? A little shiver raced down his spine, just as if he'd seen it correctly.

'I grew up here.' Sam rolled his eyes at Mick's notion to push away the hope that fluttered in his gut. 'When you said you could swim, I just assumed you meant, like properly.'

'Properly?'

Sam hummed as he held the mouthpiece for Mick. 'Put this in your mouth, wrap your lips around it, and then just breathe. Swim with the end of the tube out of the water and just breathe normally.'

Mick shook his head. 'I'm sure you didn't mean to sound quite so erotic.'

'Erotic? Me.' Sam let go of Mick and patted himself on the chest, then winked slowly, waiting until Mick grinned. His cheeks were nicely flushed.

Sam hadn't meant his comment to sound sexual but the outcome—the rosy flush on Mick's cheeks—was an excellent accidental result. 'Come on. Let's take a look around the farm.' Sam twisted in the water and leaned into the boat to grab his own snorkel. He'd done this a million times, so he had it on his face quickly, and then he pushed away from the boat and glided with easy breaststrokes along the row of oysters. After he'd given Mick enough space, he held his breath and did a roll turn, so he'd pop up facing Mick. Mick swam with cautious strokes towards him, his face aimed at the bottom of the riverbed. The main problem with doing this regularly—and since he was a toddler—was that Sam couldn't remember, or even imagine, what it would be like to experience this for the first time. He wanted to swim underneath Mick and stare at his expression to see what he might be feeling, but of course, that would, like, interrupt Mick's view of everything. So he stayed out of the way, paddling backwards, close enough to Mick to help if he needed it, but far enough away so Mick could have the full immersive experience. A school of sand whiting darted under them and Sam waited, hoping they'd be lucky enough to see a decent-sized mulloway chasing them. There were always plenty of fish species around the oysters, not because of the oysters whose hard shells protected them from being eaten, but because the infrastructure created plenty of shelter for fish. The posts, baskets and spat trays all worked in a similar fashion to an artificial reef, attracting bait species such as prawns, whiting, and other small fish.

Mick tapped him on the shoulder. 'Did you see that?' A large blue cod swam lazily underneath them.

'Yes. Isn't he beautiful?' All the smaller species that used the farm as shelter attracted larger fish who hunted them. Sam hadn't been completely kidding about sharks, although it was usually too shallow here for the bigger ones. Last year, he'd captured a brilliant image of a reef shark swimming between oyster baskets with several small fish trailing underneath the shark. It'd been one of those clear days where the sun had filtered through the water, and Sam had been on exactly the right angle to get an incredible photo. The ripple of the water above had left dappled shadows on the shark's back, resulting in one of Sam's all-time favourite images.

The smile on Mick's face, his lips stretched around the mouthpiece, was worth everything, and Sam treaded water as Mick dropped his face back into the river and kept looking. The wonder of seeing Mick's fit torso and arms stretched out in the water probably mirrored the way Mick was enjoying seeing all the different fish who lived among Sam's farm. Certainly, for Sam, seeing healthy species never got old, and no amount of gorgeous man could completely take away his geeky enjoyment of his surroundings. He rolled onto his back and stared up at the clear blue summer sky. Who was he kidding? The rash vest clung to Mick's skin, hiding nothing, and watching the water flow over Mick's muscles brought Sam's enjoyment of the farm to a new level. The clear water illuminated Mick's body, each muscle working as he glided over the surface, arms spread for balance, and his shorts were glued to his taut backside and strong thighs. Mick brushed past and Sam tried not to flinch as his touch turned Sam's thoughts into reality, but when Sam rolled around to follow Mick, all his attention was on the riverbed.

They swam together quietly, observing the fish drifting slowly down the row of oysters, for what seemed like ages before Mick lifted his head, removed the mouthpiece, and treaded water.

'Thank you so much. This is amazing.' Mick's chest heaved for breath, drawing Sam's attention to the way the water glistened on his face, and how his heavily muscled body was so bloody beautiful it made Sam's mouth dry. He wanted to peel off that rash vest and see Mick's skin, trace his fingers over each of those muscles, until they both trembled.

'It'll still be here tomorrow and the next day; you don't have to exhaust yourself.' Perhaps using sarcasm as a way of pushing away the feelings Mick aroused in his body wasn't the nicest thing. Sam exhaled and the water in front of his mouth rippled.

'True.' Mick paused, then grinned. 'Is that an invitation to do this again?'

Sam splashed water at Mick. 'Sure. Whenever you want.' Just because he was torn between wanting Mick right now and wanting to take his time, didn't mean he had to be nasty and push him away.

'Awesome. Seriously, though, how do you just tread water like that? Aren't you tired?' Mick stretched out on his back, resting on the water.

'Practice helps. Come on, let's get back to the boat and head back to shore for some lunch.' The boat wasn't too far away; they'd be able to swim there quite quickly.

Mick glanced over at the boat. 'Oh my God, we've swum for ages.'

'Not that far.'

'Are you a damned fish? I'm knackered and I thought I was fit.'

Sam raked his gaze over Mick's body. 'You do appear to be quite fit.' And strong. An itch in the back of his throat did nothing to help with Sam's current dilemma.

'Trust you to check me out when I'm too tired to do anything about it.'

Sam winked. 'It's all part of my nefarious plan.' He hauled in a deep breath. 'But honestly, if you are tired, you shouldn't push it. I'll grab the boat and bring it to you.'

'Thanks. I'll just be here trying to stay afloat.' Mick's voice did sound a little tired, with each breath more of a struggle than the one before. Sam rolled over into a dolphin dive to give himself some forward impetus and he quickly swam to the boat. If he pushed himself, the exercise would help get rid of some of the delicious tension in his limbs. He wanted to kiss Mick properly, and yet, he couldn't get rid of that nasty little voice that if he rushed into this, he'd ruin it. Therefore he punished himself by swimming as fast as he could to the boat, not bothering to take a breath, so his lungs burned and his energy became focused on staying alive.

Once they were both in the boat, Sam tossed a towel over to Mick, who draped it over those glorious strong shoulders of his. A light breeze touched Sam's cheek and he let his gaze roam over the farm; not just the assets in the water, but the shed Kiet had built, the jetty with the other boats tied up against it, and the tiny cottage he'd grown up in. They owned the paddocks surrounding the cottage and earned a little side income leasing them to a neighbour's farm for his cattle. A sense of pride in what he'd achieved together with Kiet, in the ten years since their parents had died and they'd inherited the farm, grew. The little breeze seemed to wrap itself around his shoulders and he smiled at the possibility it could be Papa's ghost. Sam didn't often feel his presence, only at times when he needed to make a decision and required a little push. Did that mean Papa liked Mick? From the way the breeze ruffled his hair then disappeared probably meant yes. His heart swelled with hope, tinged with the familiar loss that always accompanied any thoughts of his parents.

'Something has made you smile,' Mick interrupted and Sam blinked.

'Yeah, just thinking about my parents. Mum loved this place; she was born here and her father farmed this allotment before she took over.' And Papa had fallen in love with Mum and made a new home here. Papa had bought the land surrounding their cottage, little by little, growing their farm into a reasonable size until the leases gave them a good base income to hold them through a bad season. Or at least, it would have if it wasn't for Andersen and his thieving ways, but the land was still there and they'd get back in the black soon enough. Mick's earlier comment about tourists niggled at him, and Sam wondered if it might be worth getting Zoe to crunch some numbers. They could build cottages on the hillside and rent them out.

'They'd be proud of you.'

'I hope so.' Sam sighed. 'It's always tricky to think about them. Not just that they are gone—' At least gone in a physical sense, but he wasn't about to try and explain the whole Thai ghost traditions to Mick, or how he believed the stories Papa had told him and everything that went with that. Mick didn't comment, just nodded, his amber brown eyes encouraging.

'I was only sixteen when they died, and I can't help wonder if I've idealised my memories. Like, I live in the same small cottage I grew up in, and it can't have been easy to live there with three kids.'

'Three?'

Sam held his breath until the old hurt faded enough for him to speak. 'My name means "three" in Thai. Papa thought it was hilarious because my name sounds so boringly Australian, and yet it has a Thai meaning. You know, like, because I'm the youngest of three kids.' He felt like he'd explained that simple concept in the most convoluted manner, yet it reflected the tangle of his brain.

'Oh?' The confusion in Mick's voice said enough, but thankfully he didn't push for more. Sam closed his eyes; the worst part was that he couldn't remember Nok at all. All he knew of his sister was from photos; he had no recollection of her voice or anything real.

'My sister, Nok, left home when I was a toddler, and—' Sam shook his head as heat formed behind his eyes. *Left home* was the euphemism his parents had used for as long as he could remember. 'I'm sorry. I guess I just wonder about my parents and how they coped with that. It can't have been easy, and I don't really remember. Kiet says that they stayed in touch with her for a few years, but I'm not sure if that's true or if I just want it to be true. Because if it's not true, that means...' Sam's breath shook as if he'd been the one who'd swum too far in waters too deep. 'I don't understand why I don't remember my parents being sad, or arguing about why she left, or anything. I mean, there's a lot I don't know and I think I've just made my memories of them all happy. Is that fair? Does that even make sense?'

'Why would they argue? You must have a reason to think they might, otherwise you wouldn't doubt your memories.'

Sam shrugged. 'I don't know. Am I so self-absorbed that I didn't notice their pain? And I mean, there's a good chance Nok isn't even alive.'

'What?' Mick almost shouted. 'When you said she left, I assumed she was a lot older than you. Not that.'

'I asked Kiet ages ago and he said he didn't know what happened to her. That she just disappeared.' As a kid, Sam had learned not to ask Mum about it, because she always closed herself off and answered with 'she left' as if that ended the conversation. Papa was more circumspect about it, and yet vague enough that Sam was left with virtually no understanding of the truth.

Mick sat rigid and still, his eyes narrow as if he was thinking through a bunch of things. 'Okay, I've seen a lot a bad things in my work, but I've also seen some amazing things, and I want you to know that there is hope. It could be that Nok needed to forge her own life...'

Sam opened his mouth, then pinched his lips together to let Mick finish. Nok's name meant 'bird' and the idea that she had flown away to create her own life was too tempting to hold onto forever. If an idea could give him a hug, that was it.

'Which meant arguing with your parents. But you've also said that you think they might have kept in touch with her. Is it possible that they kept a connection to her, and it simply got lost when they died?'

Why hadn't Sam ever realised that? 'It is possible.' He rubbed his temple. 'But that doesn't explain why she hasn't called or visited us.'

Mick nodded. 'And that's why you can't help but wonder if your memories of your parents are flawed.'

'Yes.' Sam gasped. 'Yes, because if it was all as nice and perfect as I remember, why hasn't Nok come home? I'm stuck in a loop where my memories are of this ideal childhood that was happy and light, and yet there are facts that I'm missing. Obviously it can't have been all good, or she wouldn't have left. Or she might have come home.' Whenever Sam thought about, he could only come up with two options—either she didn't come home because she was dead, or because his memories were wrong and his parents weren't lovely—and he hated both those choices.

'I don't know the answer to that. People are often more complicated than they seem. There is one thing I do know, and that is that it's possible to have a loving relationship that survives bad things.' Mick pressed his finger to the corner of his eye.

'You do?'

'Back in Croatia during the war, terrible things happened to my parents. That's why they left and came here as refugees. But you know what?'

'What?' Sam couldn't imagine how scary it would be to live as a civilian during a war. Whatever he thought about his memories of his childhood, he knew one thing—they'd been poor and potentially not as happy as he wanted to remember, but he'd been safe. Perhaps he should just treasure his memories of his childhood and stop stressing about the other possibilities when he couldn't ever have enough information to answer all his questions.

'My parents found a way to keep loving each other, and me, despite all of that. And that gives me hope that people can be messy or hurt by the world, and keep their love strong. It doesn't always work out—' Mick's breath hitched '—but it did for my parents.'

Sam let Mick's words wash over him, in the same way the river soothed him on a hot day, and hoped Mick was right. Sam hoped his parents weren't devastated by Nok leaving—that she was living the life she needed to, out there, somewhere—and that his parents had continued loving each other, working together, and that his memories of Papa standing on the wharf laughing at something Mum had said were real.

'Your memories are real, because they are yours.' Mick reached out and placed his hand gently on Sam's thigh. It would be so tempting to stay still and let the warm comfort from Mick's touch grow until it became desire. Thoughts of kissing Mick were never far away, especially after watching him swim, and his touch only increased the tingle on Sam's lips. He couldn't. Not now. Not while his head was a complete mess.

'Thank you.' He turned on the engine and drove the boat back to the wharf, blaming the wind for the way his eyes leaked with water. If only Mick was correct and he could banish this doubt that he'd fashioned an upbeat view of his childhood out of hope, not reality. The rushing air filled his lungs and he realised that both could be true. His parents could be complicated—they could have created a good childhood for him with moments of happiness—and they could have been hurt by the way Nok ran away from home. He'd spent years worried that Nok was dead, because she never called home, yet there was a logic to Mick's comment about losing touch after his parents died. Maybe she was fine and she didn't want to be found, which brought a different sort of pain. What had he done wrong to make her leave him? Her little brother. Didn't that count for something? They were almost at the jetty, and he blinked as he slowed the boat. Maybe it wasn't about him at all. That'd been the crux of Lizzy's complaints. He internalised everyone else's problems and made them his fault; that was one of the reasons why she'd told him to grow up. 'Not everything is about you., The other thing she hated was his enjoyment of SDH, but he'd never regret that, not when it had connected him with Mick. He probably should thank his cousins sometime, for introducing him to the game.

'Thanks, Mick.' Sam cut the engine and threw the rope over the mooring on the jetty. 'Let's go and have a beer, and maybe a snack if you're hungry. We'll have to sit outside, because Kiet will be getting ready to cook dinner and he doesn't like it when I get in his way in the kitchen.' Now there were three of them in the house, they each had to cook less often, but on his nights Kiet always went overboard to impress Zoe.

'Kiet cooks?'

Sam chuckled. 'I know he tries to be a grumpy old man, but for a long time it was just me and him. If we didn't learn to cook, we didn't eat.'

Mick nodded. 'Makes sense. I live alone and have to feed myself too.'

'No microwaved meals for one while you give up strategic space on SDH?' Sam teased. He didn't like eating while on his computer—crumbs in the keyboard was the worst—but he often just made sandwiches for dinner because he couldn't be bothered cooking. Or more accurately, he hated cleaning up afterwards since they didn't have a dishwasher or any of that fancy stuff.

'Is it okay if I stay for lunch?'

'Of course. You are my guest. Let me feed you.'

Mick's eyebrows raised. 'Tempting.'

Sam jumped out of the boat and busied himself with tying it up properly, so Mick wouldn't see the way his cheeks burned with heat. All he had to do was get through lunch and then Mick would leave to go to work, and Sam could spend some time examining his head without distraction. Gorgeous, funny, sensible distraction. At least Kiet's presence might just save Sam from himself and the temptation to follow his desires.

***

Hours later when Mick had left to go to work, Sam poked his head into Kiet's room. 'Hey Kiet?'

'Yeah?'

'Do you know what happened with Nok? Is she okay?'

Kiet shook his head. 'I don't know much. I remember that Nok wanted to do a summer holiday job, and our parents stopped her. But I don't recall the details. I wish I did.'

'It's not your responsibility to know. You were just a kid.' Sam paused. Kiet had been a kid, just like him. 'We should look her up online.' Their surname, Viravaidya, was quite distinctive. Sam had never been tempted to do that before—just in case he found nothing; would he rather know even if it was bad news?

Kiet growled under his breath. 'I've tried that.'

'Fair enough.' Sam knew he'd try later once Kiet had left his room. He didn't want to disparage his brother, but he spent a ton more time online than Kiet, and surely his google skills had to be stronger. 'Hey, thanks. Do you think our parents were happy together after...?'

'After Nok left? Yes and no. There were moments of sadness, like on her birthday, or on the anniversary of the day she left, and at other random times, but mostly our parents loved each other and worked well together.'

'I hope that's true.'

'Why do you ask?'

Sam inhaled deeply. 'I had an excellent childhood, and yet, there is this whole mystery, and I've been wondering lately if I'd forgotten things. Like, did I just invent a happy childhood because I wanted that?'

Kiet rubbed Sam on the shoulder. 'No. We had a good childhood. Mum and Papa did a really good job sheltering us from their problems. It wasn't until after they died, that I realised that the farm was in a difficult position financially. They were doing okay but one bad season might have ruined them.'

'Oh?' Sam had always assumed the land Papa had purchased helped offset the risk of losses, but as he thought back over it, often that land had stayed fallow. The oyster farm took a lot of hours to keep productive, leaving little time to deal with their land, hence the arrangement with the neighbouring cattle farmer.

'I guess Mum didn't know any different. She'd grown up here, and it was probably like that all the time. It wasn't until we had your expertise that we were able to do better future planning. They'd be proud of you, Sam.'

Sam nodded, his throat thick. After a moment, Kiet turned to leave and Sam coughed gently to remove the burr from the back of his throat.

'Hey Kiet.'

'Yeah?'

'Thank you for everything.' For sending him away for the last couple of years of high school, for making Papa's land purchases productive to mitigate their financial risk, for reminding him that his childhood was good. That wasn't just his imagination. Now it was up to him to grow up and become a person worthy of his brother's love and hard work.

Chapter 8

For the next week, Mick was haunted by the idea of flawed memories. Little snippets of conversations with Sam kept rolling around his head, and he wondered if he'd been wrong to keep forgiving Xavier. Now he'd been away from Xavier for over a year, he couldn't help but wonder if he'd lost himself by falling for Xavier's charm. It was difficult to think he might have been wrong about Xavier. Had Xavier really walked all over him, and had he just ... *let* him do that? He couldn't recall the details and he was left with a deep sense of loss. Not for Xavier, but for himself. He'd come here for the promotion, not to get away, and yet Sam's comments made him wonder if he'd been lying to himself about that. Had he come here to Rainbow Cove to find himself again? Who was he when he wasn't pandering to Xavier's moods?

All that introspection disappeared when he slept. Memories of Sam's lean body moving in the water as if he belonged there, mingled with elements of fantasy from SDH, haunted him, until he dreamed of mermen chasing him through his sleep. Sea creatures with Sam's face and cheeky grin. It was probably because he spent a couple of hours after each shift hanging out on SDH chatting to Sam and expanding their joint empire. Yesterday, they'd dealt with a threat from a newcomer who tried to hook up to their discs and invade.

Mick yawned—yeah, he'd spent too much time online yesterday morning. He had the next few days off, and then would be back on days. This schedule was the worst thing about working in a smaller town. No one wanted the night shift permanently—or the day shift, to be fair—so everyone did four days on, four nights on, then four days and nights off, on rotation. Nights were full of more interesting work, while days tended to be a lot of boring transfer work, but Mick found that night shift was much tougher on his body, and more importantly, on his burgeoning relationship with Sam. He glanced at his clock. Sam would likely be online now; he usually was at this time of the morning, which made sense to Mick now that he'd been at the farm. Sam got up early to work and beat the heat of the day, then came inside to eat and hang out online for a while before heading back to work once it cooled off again.

Velebit: I hope this isn't too forward, but I want to see you again.

Crassostrea: Did we just time travel? Too forward. Mate. Just ask.

Velebit: *blushes* Would you like to have dinner with me this week? It's my weekend, then I'm on days.

Crassostrea: Dinner sounds good. I've been wanting to try Christophe's new summer menu.

Velebit: Christophe?

Crassostrea: I forgot you were new to town. Christophe is the chef at the Rainbow Cove resort.

Velebit: So a fancy dinner then?

Crassostrea: I'll pay. I get a discount anyway since we supply their oysters.

Velebit: I asked. I can pay. Friday?

Crassostrea: Ok. I'll make a booking.

Velebit: Do we need a booking? Are they that busy?

Crassostrea: Friday night in summer. Yeah, they'll be pretty busy with people who've arrived for a weekend at the resort. We could go another night if you don't want crowds.

Velebit: Nah. I want to be seen in public with you. Mick shouldn't really push Sam given how much Sam had talked about wanting to take his time, especially not now Mick had started to examine his own Sydney past.

Crassostrea: Is that code for 'please be my boyfriend?,

Velebit: If you want it to be.

Crassostrea added a gif that said 'thoughts loading'. Mick swallowed. Crap, he'd screwed up and pushed Sam too hard. He tucked his hands into his lap, so he didn't reply with something desperate. Or anything at all. Mick's stomach clenched, the same way it used to whenever Xavier returned. The taut sensation unsettled him because he'd never realised that it meant he was worried. He'd always thought it was happy nerves.

Crassostrea: I'd like to say yes, but I'm worried about rushing into this.

Velebit: Valid. A sudden cold chill washed over Mick. He needed to wait too. It didn't matter that they'd known each other online for months before they met in real life, or that they'd spent a lot of time together recently without moving into relationship status. Sam had been open about his concerns, and if it mattered to Sam, then it mattered to Mick. More than that, Mick knew he needed to reassess his past.

Crassostrea: Are you just saying that to get into my pants?

Mick smiled. If only it was that simple. He added a gif of someone saying 'hey'.

Velebit: If I only wanted to get into your pants, we'd have already been there.

Crassostrea: Arrogant ☺

Three dots appeared and Mick waited for Sam to finish typing. It was taking him ages, so either he was typing and deleting, or he was writing a damned essay.

Crassostrea: But also ... valid. The real problem is that I like you and I don't want to mess that up. If that's what Sam finally decided to send, Mick wanted to know what he'd deleted.

Velebit: Liking me is a problem? Xavier used to say something similar, as a joke, that he liked Mick too much and it was a problem because he needed him. The cold surrounding his body dropped a few degrees. He wasn't sure he wanted to read what Sam had to say, but Sam was nothing like Xavier. Nothing at all.

Crassostrea: Yes, because it complicates everything. If it was just sex, then we'd be done already.

Mick's mouth dried. Had he misread everything? *Velebit: ok? Sex is not that complicated, and why are you having sex with people you don't like?*

Crassostrea: Umm, refer to our discussion, like, yesterday about your ex's.

Mick grimaced. Yesterday, they'd chatted about some of his life in Sydney. The sanitised version, sans Xavier.

Velebit: Yes, that makes me a hypocrite. I told you I'm done with temporary pleasure. He'd deliberately steered clear of talking about Xavier, focusing instead on the one-night stands he'd had before then. Until Sam had told him off for dismissing the concerns of domestic abuse survivors, Mick had never imagined he was one. He'd let Xavier tell him it was his fault they broke up, that Xavier couldn't nurse him after his accident, not that Xavier left when Mick wasn't available for sex anytime Xavier wanted. That couldn't be right though. Xavier had gone to help his sister. Back then, Mick had been annoyed that Xavier's sister was more important than him, but now he couldn't help wondering if Xavier even had a sister. If he did, he'd never mentioned her name. Was it just another one of Xavier's excuses?

How could he talk to Sam about Xavier and the whole mess after the factory explosion if he didn't know how he felt about it himself?

Crassostrea: What we have feels real and I don't want to mess that up.

The cold disappeared and Mick's whole body suddenly felt lighter. Mick took a screenshot and saved it. He wanted to keep that statement. Actually, he wanted to keep the glow it gave him. Sam cared enough about him to ensure he was ready to have a relationship with him. The irony in Sam wanting to take it slow when Mick had so many conflicted emotions around relationships wasn't lost on him. Sam was doing this for himself. He had no idea Mick needed time to figure out the uncomfortable truth of his past.

Velebit: Thank you. Dinner at 7?

Crassostrea: Deal.

Velebit: I'll pick you up at 6.30.

Crassostrea: Will you now?

Velebit: Hey. I'm not offering so I can I ask you into bed afterwards.

Crassostrea: That's a shame.

Velebit: What? Mick leaned over his keyboard, swaying slightly at the apparent change of heart. He couldn't live his life like this again. All the little pieces suddenly painted a picture and he knew the truth. Xavier had abused him, in subtle ways that undermined him until he wasn't sure what was real and what wasn't.

*Crassostrea: *sighs dramatically* See — I don't know what I want.*

Velebit: Dinner first. We can work the rest out later. He didn't feel as calm as his typed words read, but he knew it was true: they could work the rest out later.

***

From the way Sam tugged at his collar as they drove into the carpark at the Rainbow Cove Resort, it was obvious to Mick that he was uncomfortable. Mick had been there too many times and he would never wish that on anyone else. Over the last few days, much more had become clear and Mick realised he needed to see a therapist to really put his time with Xavier into the past. He didn't want to repeat the same mistakes, and he sure as heck didn't want to push Sam like he'd been pushed. If Sam was uncomfortable, they could stop now before they started. He never felt that old uncertainty around Sam. Being with Xavier had meant being prepared for when Xavier might suddenly change his mind and ruin all his plans just for shits and giggles. And because Sam was up-front, consistent and, quite frankly, completely opposite to Xavier, Mick wasn't going to do anything that even hinted at that unnerving imbalance.

'Hey Sam?'

'Yeah?' Sam shot him a glance then looked out the window again.

'Please tell me what's wrong.'

Sam cleared his throat. 'Marandowie is a small town...'

When he didn't elaborate, Mick frowned. 'And?'

'Oh, that's right, you're a city boy. You have no clue about small towns and how the grapevine works.'

'The what?'

Sam heaved out a loud sigh. 'Like, gossip. Once we walk inside, the whole town is going to know we had a date together; and then someone will remember we had dinner together in the pub, and the next thing you know everyone will be speculating on when we'll be getting married...'

'Is that a bad thing? At least we can get married in Australia now.'

Sam sighed again. 'Oh God. And then there will be the people who will be pearl-clutching shocked. "OMG, I didn't know Sam was Gay" with a capital G. I really don't want them turning up at the farm trying to convert me or some shit.'

'Hold on.' Mick parked the car and turned off the engine. 'Are you telling me you aren't out? We don't have to do this.'

'Is anyone ever out all the time?' Sam scoffed.

'True. It annoys me on TV when people have a big coming out moment and then it's never mentioned again, when the reality is that you have to decide whether or not to mention it with every person you meet. Is it any of their business? Is it going to matter? Why should I hide myself? But what if it's not safe?'

Sam reached over and laid his palm against Mick's cheek. 'All of that. I'm not overly worried about people thinking I'm queer. It's not an issue. I mean, it is, because small-town gossip can be irritating. But I am queer; I have friends here who won't care, and I'm comfortable with myself and with people knowing.'

'Okay?' Mick wanted to lean against Sam's hand; the calluses from his work-roughened hands were rough against his freshly shaven cheek, a delightful contrast that made Mick wonder what it would feel like to have Sam's hands stroke his body.

'I think I'm just overthinking this. You know, inventing problems where there aren't any.'

Mick turned so he could kiss Sam's palm. 'I want you to be comfortable.' In all ways—with Mick and in public. 'Please don't out yourself for me.'

'Thank you. It'll be fine. It's just that I've never really been open about myself in town.'

A fragment of a memory made the hairs on Mick's arms raise a little. 'But you said your ex was a local too.'

Sam dropped his hand and shrank backwards. 'Is now a good time to tell you that I'm bisexual? My ex, Lizzy, was ... is, she's a woman. I've never been with a man in town, I mean, like, I've been with men but when I was at uni and it was easier in the city.' Sam scrambled his words, rushing through them, obviously nervous and Mick wanted to pull him into a reassuring hug. To reassure them both. Sam hadn't lied to him.

Now that he'd started to understand how many ways Xavier had messed with him, he'd become ultra-aware of the same tactics. It'd been Sam's brutal honesty at their first dinner at the pub that had put Mick at ease, and he hadn't even known why.

'And this will be the first time it's obvious that you are bi; hence the "omg I didn't know Sam was gay" comment.' It had taken him years to work up the courage to tell his parents he was gay. Xavier had done it for him without permission; another way he'd undermined Mick. Luckily, Mick's parents had been amazing about it without an ounce of rejection, treating the whole revelation as if it were fine. It hadn't been so simple for many of Mick's friends and his veins overflowed with empathy for Sam. If only he could wrap Sam in a big hug and tell him it would be okay, even though it probably wouldn't. Even in Sydney, where people were more used to meeting all types of folks, Mick had dealt with the occasional shitty homophobic comment. Was it wrong to assume it would be worse in a small town?

'Yeah. That's it...' Sam breathed in, his nostrils flaring. 'I guess I am outing myself tonight to the town by turning up here with you.'

'That's a pretty big deal. If you aren't ready, we can wait for another night.'

'Thank you, but no. When my parents died, Kiet sent me away to boarding school. I'd been getting bullied a bit—the usual crap—and he was worried it would get worse with the grief and everything. I agreed at the time because it felt good to be away from all the snide gossip and bullshit, but I'm older now. I can deal with their ignorant comments. I refuse to run; besides I have my sister-in-law Zoe now. She's dealt with this town before when her sister Jade came out.'

'Was that bad?' Mick recalled the conversation from their first meeting in the pub, but they hadn't really gone into how bigoted this town was generally.

Sam waggled his head and bit his bottom lip. 'Their parents and the church were awful with a capital A, but most of the rest of the town were amazing. People offered their homes for them to stay in when Jade was kicked out by her parents.' He sighed. 'Okay, that helped.'

Mick leaned forward and kissed Sam on the forehead. 'And you have me to support you too. But please ... anytime it gets too much, tell me and we'll leave.'

'A little part of me wants to go inside and listen to the ignorant few try and puzzle it out.'

Mick chuckled and lifted his voice in a snide mockery of a bigot. 'Isn't that Sam? Weird place to go to dinner with friends.'

'Oh it's so niiice—' Sam drew out the "nice" with a ton of sarcasm '—to see him getting out again after Lizzy broke up with him. I felt so sorry for him, blah blah.'

'I'll just have to kiss you to make sure they get absolutely the right idea.'

Sam laughed, and the lump in Mick's gut eased. 'I'd rather you kiss me because you want to, not because of some petty notion to annoy the bigots in town.'

'Trust me. I've been wanting to kiss you for weeks now. When I do—' Mick paused deliberately '—it'll be because I want to kiss you.' His mouth watered at the thought. He'd imagined kissing Sam so many times. A proper kiss. He swallowed.

'I've made up my mind.' Sam leaped out of the car.

Mick scrambled to follow. 'Yes?' If Sam wanted a kiss, why leave the car?

'I'm only going inside if you hold my hand. Let's give the gossipers something to talk about.' The determination in Sam's voice washed over Mick like a waterfall on a sticky hot day. Sam squared his shoulders and held his head high.

'That's the spirit. Why let them dictate the story about you?'

Sam laughed. 'Calm down. It's only small-town gossip, not like national media. But yeah, I get your point. I should choose how they see me; not let them spend the evening texting each other with made-up nonsense.'

'If what you say about small towns is true, they'll probably do that too.'

'True. Or no one from town will be there tonight and I will have stressed about nothing.' Sam held out his hand for Mick, and together they walked towards the front door of the resort. After a few minutes, they were led to their table overlooking the bay and Mick reluctantly released Sam's hand so they could be seated. A server appeared beside the table before Mick could smile at Sam and say something bland, like *well that wasn't too bad.*

'Sam. How's things?'

'Celia? Celia Chan? I'm good, how are you?'

'I'm good.'

'How long have you worked here? I thought you were in Sydney.'

The waitress lifted her chin a little. 'My mum is sick. I had to come home, and I was lucky to get this job.'

'Oh, that's terrible.' From the look on Sam's face, Mick knew he was thinking about his own parents.

'Yeah, well. That's life, isn't it.'

'I'm so sorry to hear about your mum, Celia. I know how close you both were. Are.' The shared look between Sam and Celia spoke of years of knowledge about each other, and Mick started to understand the whole small-town thing Sam had mentioned. 'How's Eddie?' It wasn't just that everyone gossiped about each other, but they'd known each other their whole lives and had all this history together. He was the interloper, from out of town, who didn't quite belong. At least, not yet. He'd like to belong with Sam, and that meant fitting in with the whole town.

Celia blew out a short breath. 'Eddie's good. Busy, you know, with the farm and stuff.'

'Yeah, I know what that's like. I should give him a bell and go fishing sometime.'

'I'm sure he'd like that. Who is your friend?'

Sam pointed across the table. 'This is Mick. He's the new paramedic in town.'

'Hi.' Mick reached across the table and laid his hand on Sam's wrist and Sam smiled gently at him.

Celia glanced back and forth between them, frowning. 'So are you guys a thing?'

Mick nodded, not daring to glance at Sam in case he disagreed, even though he hadn't pulled his arm away from Mick's touch. 'Yeah.'

'Working quickly, huh, Sam? Gotta grab him before anyone else in town does?' Celia's teasing had an undercurrent that Mick didn't like. What was she getting at?

'We've known each other for a while.' Mick jumped in to defend Sam. Confusingly, Sam glared at him.

Celia paused for a moment, her gaze flicking back and forth between them. 'Like, while you were going out with Lizzy? Dude, that's not cool.'

Sam growled under his breath. 'No. No, not while I was going out with Lizzy. I would never. Why does everyone think that being bi means you are a cheater? It's such crap.'

'You're bi? Oh, of course you are, if you are here with a bloke. Duh.' Celia stared at Sam with wide-open eyes, while Sam squirmed in his seat.

'Is that a problem?' Mick didn't bother to hide his disdain.

'Is what a problem?' Celia frowned. 'I'm so confused. Like, I heard that Lizzy cheated on you with some bloke she hooked up with at Christmas, and now this. Mate, your sex life is the most entertaining topic in town.'

Sam's jaw tightened. 'I'm so glad my life keeps everyone amused.'

'So she did cheat on you, not you cheating on her?'

Sam rolled his eyes. 'No one cheated on anyone. There's no interesting gossip here. My life is nowhere near as exciting as people make it out to be! Lizzy and I broke up a few weeks before Christmas, and this is literally the first date I've been on since.'

'Second.' Mick had fond memories of their dinner in the pub, especially Sam's cute awkwardness, complete honesty, and the way his skin felt when he brushed Sam's forehead.

'Mick, that's not helping. First official date. Before that, Mick and I were just friends, and I know nothing about Lizzy's new bloke. I genuinely hope she's happy.'

'Okay, man, don't get your pants twisted up.' Celia shrugged one shoulder. 'I'm just asking a few questions, like anyone would.'

'It's fine. You're right, there's not much to do around here. If it was you, I'd want to know all the deets too.' Sam grinned at Celia. 'I hope your mum gets better.'

'Thanks. I appreciate it. You guys ready to order?'

Mick flicked his gaze over the menu. 'Sam, do you want some oysters to start? Or are you bored with eating them?'

Sam grinned. 'They are the ones from our farm. I'd love to taste what Christophe has done with them.'

'And they are an aphrodisiac.' Celia winked at Sam. The coy look on Sam's face matched the delightful blush spreading over his cheeks.

'Cool. I'll have a pint of the local IPA. What do you want to drink, Mick?'

'I'll have a lemon, lime and bitters. I'm driving.' Mick never drank when he was driving. He'd seen way too many road accidents to take any chances with his own life. If that made him a boring old man, he'd be happy to say he'd always been boring. Why take the risk when it was so easily avoided?

'I'll be back soon.'

'Thanks, Celia, and hey...'

'Yeah?'

'Look after yourself.' Sam's empathy for Celia's situation without any details, and while fielding so many personal questions about himself, was outstanding.

'So you guys went to school together?' Mick stroked his thumb over Sam's wrist, subtly checking his pulse, which was slower than Mick's own. Touching Sam always increased his heartrate.

Sam nodded. 'Yeah. Celia was a year below me, but Marandowie High is a pretty small school. We all knew each other. Her brother Eddie was a year above me. He's still at their family farm; we go fishing together sometimes.'

Sam sighed. 'Damn you. You've distracted me—I should have dropped by to have a beer with him or something. I haven't seen Eddie for ages. I didn't even know their mum was sick.'

'Don't you dare blame yourself.' Mick was puzzled by the way Sam seemed to be disappointed in himself.

'What?'

'You've spent half our evening together railing against the gossip in the town, and then being subject to it, but now you are ... what? Guilty, because you haven't been listening to the same gossip that irritates you?'

'It doesn't have to be logical. Eddie is my friend and his mum is sick.'

It wasn't guilt, it was friendship and empathy. Mick tried to look reassuring as he smiled. 'You still can visit. Go tomorrow.'

Sam nodded. 'That's a good idea. I'll do that.'

Chapter 9

Sam tried to ignore the way his hand tingled from Mick's touch. Chatting with Celia actually eased his concerns about the Marandowie grapevine. People were already talking about him; he may as well give them something concrete to talk about. Another waiter arrived with their drinks, and Mick lifted his hand to take his lemon, lime and bitters.

'Cheers. Here's to a nice evening out, to our friendship, and the exploration of more.' Mick winked at him, and Sam had to pinch his lips together to stop spluttering out a laugh.

'Right back at you with your fancy pub squash.' He picked up his beer and clinked his glass with Mick. Sam sipped his beer slowly, unsure about what to say next. Talking to Mick was always easier online when he couldn't see him. Why was it he always got tongue-tied around Mick's handsome face?

'I don't, by the way.'

Sam put his beer down. 'You don't, what?'

'I don't believe that being bisexual makes someone automatically a cheater.'

The tension in Sam's shoulders started to relax. 'Thank you.' He hadn't broached the subject with Mick, or Lizzy, or anyone, but he was glad it had come up, because it would be a deal-breaker in a relationship over the long term. His spine stiffened—long term? Yes, that was what he wanted with Mick, which was why this was important to him. They might have only met IRL a few times but each time reinforced their online friendship with an extra kick of lust.

'The stereotype makes no sense to me,' Mick said. 'Unless people assume that every time someone appreciates another person, then they are cheating. Is it cheating when I say a bloke is well-built, or hot as heck, or has an amazing aesthetic? No. I don't think so. Why should the gender of the person you notice make any difference? It shouldn't.'

'Um, wow. Yes, obviously I agree with you.'

Mick smiled, his eyes full of warmth. 'But?'

'I didn't quite expect the detailed defence.' The gentle buzz in his veins—always present when he was near Mick—started to increase, and he was sorely tempted to abandon their dinner and drag Mick home to his bed. The instinct made him pause because that was exactly how he'd messed up in the past. At the risk of boring himself with his own repetitiveness, he needed to take his time. Celia saved him from further speech by arriving with the oysters.

'Oysters four ways; we have natural, with mignonette sauce, with tarragon butter, and lastly

Christophe's special cucumber and watermelon relish.'

Sam hummed appreciatively under his breath. 'They look amazing.'

'Shall I give you some time to indulge, or are you ready to order?' Celia asked.

Sam didn't want her to come back to their table again; he'd rather spend his time with Mick without constant interruptions. 'What do you recommend? I'll have that.'

'You could try our degustation?'

'Your what?' Trust a Frenchman to have a fancy name for his food. Sam would have to tease Christophe about it next time he saw him.

Celia spread her hands out in the air. 'It's a tasting menu. A series of small dishes to reflect the entirety of Christophe's skill as a chef and created from local produce so it also tells a story about the local environment. The oysters are the first dish if you choose that option.'

'That sounds exactly like what I want. Locally sourced produce, crafted into something special.' From the look Mick gave him, Sam had surprised him with his choice. 'What? I'm not just a hick farmer.' Just because he hadn't known degustation meant tasting menu...

'Obviously.' Mick looked up at Celia. 'Let's have the degustation. Thank you.'

'Do you want matching wines, Sam? I know your date isn't drinking.' In the carpark, they'd teased each other about this being a proper date, and yet to have Celia suggest it so casually made it real.

Sam brushed away the niggle of fear to focus on the important question. 'Mick, is it weird for me to do the matching wines when you aren't?'

'No, it's fine.'

'Okay, let's have the whole experience then. I trust Christophe.' It was true; Christophe might be a bit too fancy with his food, but he was a good mate and that mattered more than anything else. Celia nodded and slipped away from the table.

'You trust Christophe?' Did Mick mean to sound like he didn't say *but not me?*

'With the food, obvs. I trust you with me, that's a whole different thing.'

'You do?'

Sam blinked twice. 'How can you doubt it? I'm here, in public, on a date with you, with the whole town talking about me. Which—' Sam held up one hand to stop Mick from talking '—they all will be now. I'd bet Celia is texting her brother Eddie, and some of her friends too, and then it'll be everywhere. But it doesn't matter because I'm choosing to be here. I want everyone to know that I'm happy, that breaking up with Lizzy didn't leave me sad and hiding on the farm. That I'm bisexual and damned proud of being me.' And with that grand speech—and to hide the tremor in his hand—Sam picked up a naked oyster and let it slip into his mouth. It was good ... but not as good as fresh off the farm. He could tell that they'd been harvested this morning and had sat around on ice all day.

'Are you alright? I mean, I completely agree with everything you said, but your expression?'

'It's just the oyster, it's old.'

'Old?'

'Yeah, about twelve hours since it was harvested.'

'You can taste that?' Mick paused and gave his head a slight shake. 'Of course you can. It's your job.'

Sam picked up one of the ones with tiny pieces of watermelon and cucumber scattered over the oyster. 'Perhaps one with a relish will be better as it will have a different balance of flavours and I might not notice?'

'Perhaps.' Mick's mouth opened slightly and Sam suddenly wanted to feed the oyster to Mick rather than eat it himself. He picked up another naked one in his other hand and leaned forward.

'Open.' Sam slid the oyster off the shell into Mick's mouth—no wonder people said oysters were an aphrodisiac. Seeing Mick's lips close around the soft flesh of the oyster was bloody erotic, and sent a shiver of delight rushing down Sam's spine.

'That's good.' The huskiness in Mick's voice dismissed the obvious joke about Mick not being able to tell the freshness, or the response inspired by seeing him eat an oyster Sam had grown. 'Here, try this one.'

Sam opened his mouth and Mick fed him one of the relish ones. The sharp sweetness of the watermelon cut through the salty tang of the oyster and added a bit of crunchy texture to the slippery meat. 'Okay. Christophe is a genius. That was amazing.'

'As was the look on your face.' There was a glow to Mick's face, with patches of heightened colour, and Sam knew how he'd look in bed. If he wanted to go slowly, Sam was going about this completely the wrong way. Sam closed his eyes to savour the notion. Maybe it was time to take the next step and stop fighting this incredible attraction. An attraction that had grown from friendship and now threatened to be something more. No, not threatened ... *beckoned*. Sam was drawn to Mick like a Christmas beetle to the porch light on a hot summer's night.

'Careful.'

'Excuse me?' Sam stared at Mick.

'You're about to drop that one.' Mick glanced down at Sam's hand, and Sam realised he'd completely forgotten he was holding an oyster in his fingers. Perhaps it was his callused hands' familiarity with the shell that meant he'd lost track of the oyster. Or perhaps it was simply the heat in Mick's gaze. He lifted the shell and slipped the oyster into his mouth.

'I must get this recipe from Christophe. It's incredible.'

Mick grinned. 'Do you think he'll share his secrets?'

'Maybe not. Chefs!' Sam rolled his eyes and was rewarded when Mick's grin widened. 'Shall we try the mignonette, or the tarragon butter?'

'Both.'

Sam frowned. 'Not together.'

'No, but there is no rush. Savour them.' In a few words, Mick outlined the part of the puzzle Sam had missed. He could kiss Mick without rushing the next stage. All he needed to do was savour each moment. His mouth watered and he swallowed.

'Tarragon butter, I think, then save the mignonette for last as the vinegar will cut through the butter.'

Mick's grin widened and his eye flickered with the shadow of a wink. 'I bow to your oyster expertise.'

'I wish I had a witty retort.'

'Imagine it's SDH; what would you type to me?'

Sam sighed. 'How did you know I find it easier to be funny over DMs than IRL?'

'Because I know you in both realms. You are just as cute IRL, more so because your face is quite openly expressive. It's just that it seems to take you a while to warm into your usual self when we are together.'

Sam knew why. He drew in a deep breath. 'It's because you are distractingly hot in real life. When it's just a computer and your avatar—which btw looks nothing like you—it's easier to relax and talk.'

'I'm the same person in both places.'

'I know that.' Sam didn't need to have his faint social anxiety analysed. He picked up an oyster and ate it. The blend of salty oyster meat with the richness of butter and the sharp tarragon notes was excellent. So different to the relish in both texture and flavour. Where the relish was fresh and sharp, the butter was round and wholesome.

'I wish you would share all those thoughts,' Mick said.

'But they are dull. I was just thinking about the flavour balance of the different dressings Christophe has used and how they are poles apart in style yet both exactly right to match the oyster without overwhelming the core flavour of the meat.'

Mick shook his head and sent Sam a rueful glance. 'Okay, none of that is boring.'

'It isn't?'

'No. Whenever you talk about something you care deeply about, you get this look on your face. Slightly faraway, slightly absorbed, and it's amazing to watch.'

Sam frowned. 'It's not self-centred and dorky?'

Mick's eyes widened and he held up his hand. 'Stop. Whoever told you that doesn't deserve you. I adore your thoughts, especially when you get carried away on a subject that thrills you. I'd even listen to you talk about sharks.'

'You wouldn't, though.' Sam had a hankering to show Mick his photo of the reef shark. Was that the equivalent of showing someone your etchings? Sam had come across the old-fashioned slang once when reading a historical gay novel and it had stuck with him as being ridiculously funny.

'See. You are doing it again. Thinking something, this time with a sly little grin, and not sharing it.'

Sam's cheeks heated. 'Um, yeah, that one's not safe for public.'

'Now I'm intrigued. How do you get from sharks to NSFW?'

Sam couldn't stop the laugh. 'It's you. I told you that you're distracting. Besides it was nothing.'

'Not nothing if it makes you blush like that.'

'Fine. I have a photo I took of a shark and I thought about asking you to have a look at it, because I think it's one of the best photos I've taken, and then I thought about...' Sam paused, unwilling to explain the etchings joke because it was OTT geeky.

'Yeah?'

He lowered his voice. 'Having you in my room.'

Mick's tongue darted out of his mouth and he licked his bottom lip. 'Shall we skip the rest of dinner?'

'Tempting. Very tempting. But no.' Sam knew he'd invite Mick into his room tonight, and he wanted to drag out the anticipation for as long as he could. From the way his skin felt a bit too tight, and his blood too hot for his veins, Sam knew the build-up would make tonight even better.

'Oyster?'

'Thank you. And to be clear, that's not a solid no. It's only that I want to...'

'Take your time.' Mick leaned back in his chair a bit, as if rejected.

Sam leaned forward, his elbows on the table, and purposefully rested his chin in his hands. 'Mick. Tonight, I want to invite you into my bed.'

Colour splashed over Mick's face, blotchy on his cheeks and he leaned closer to Sam. 'Oh?'

'Yes. I've had enough time. It's just that I want to savour you. I want to take my time tonight and enjoy this dinner with you. I want to spend my time with you because you've come to matter to me.'

Mick swallowed, his throat moving slowly. 'Okay.' His voice croaked huskily and Sam shivered.

'It'll be good.'

It took Mick a moment before he answered. 'No, it'll be amazing. Because you, Sam, are a brilliant man who I adore.'

Chapter 10

Mick tasted nothing for the rest of the meal. The food was probably good, judging by Sam's expressions of enjoyment. Expressions which stole Mick's ability to focus on anything else. With each tasting plate, Sam had a small glass of wine—a thimble of liquid in a tall elegant glass—and as he ate and drank, he became cuter and cuter. Looser with his tongue, and utterly adorable. For all of Sam's big talking about wanting to take Mick to his bed, Mick knew it wouldn't be tonight. Sam wasn't terribly drunk, but he was certainly too tipsy to consent properly, and Mick wanted no regrets between them.

'You gotta try this chocolate dessert. It's sinful.' Sam leaned forward with a spoonful of the dessert perched precariously in his fingers. There was something delightful about a faintly intoxicated Sam, except it reminded Mick that he was painfully sober.

'I know. I have the exact same dessert.'

A frown flashed on Sam's face. 'Oh, so you do. Am I very drunk?'

'More like a little tipsy, not overly drunk.'

'Damn. I didn't mean to do this, but all the wines were so delicious and you know, Celia promised they'd match the food perfectly and they do. They really do, it's a skill to create that. And anyway, how could I be drunk? Like every dish only had a splash of wine with it, and these glasses are so massive, it seems like every sip they're like, I don't know. What was I saying?'

'Sam.' Mick grinned. 'It's okay. I'll take you home to bed.'

'That sounds amazing. I've wanted to kiss you for like weeks now. Why haven't I done that? Bloody Lizzy; I think she really confused me, because we jumped into bed together too fast and then it all kind of went wrong, but the sex was still good.' Sam clamped his hand over his mouth. 'Oops.'

'It's okay.'

'It's not okay. She told me I needed to grow up, but it wasn't all my fault, but it was, you know. Like, that wasn't the first time I'd slept with someone too fast and then messed it up, but with you...' Sam waved the spoon of chocolate around, and Mick gently moved Sam's hand back down to the table before chocolate cake and sauce scattered all over the crisp white tablecloth. Just like the casual loose movement of Sam's hands, Mick's head was spinning at Sam's revelations.

'With me?'

'Yes, I'm with you. Why do you ask?'

Mick chuckled and Sam giggled in response. 'Sam, I'm taking you home.'

'Good. I thought you'd never ask.' He tried to stand up, then sat down hard. 'Shit. I'm drunk. How did that happen? I'm never drunk. What did you do to me?'

'Nothing. It's the tasting wines that you had with each meal.'

'Oh yeah. I don't think that was a good idea. Why do I always make bad choices without thinking them through? How am I going to get home now? I can't sleep here.'

Mick shook his head. There was something in there about Sam's apparent bad choices that he'd need to keep close until they could talk about it in the morning, but he dealt with the immediate issue first. 'I drove you here and I'll drop you home.'

'Okay. That's good. Thanks.'

Mick stood up and held out his hand for Sam. 'Come on, let's get you home and you can sleep this off.' Sam jumped up out of his chair and nearly knocked them both over with his uncoordinated enthusiasm.

'Thanks. You're the best. Also, did you know that you are very strong?' Sam held on tight to Mick's biceps, and Mick sighed, unable to enjoy this. If Sam remembered this tomorrow, he'd be so embarrassed.

'Sam. Come with me.' He needed to get Sam home, where he could be cute and giggly without anyone able to see and gossip about him. Mick tucked Sam's arm around his elbow and walked them both out of the restaurant. As he paid at the front desk, Sam lay his head on Mick's shoulder and sighed. Damn him for being the cutest lightweight drunk ever. The sum of the tasting wines would be only a couple of standard glasses, spread over the ten different dishes of the degustation.

'Thank you for dinner.'

Sam lifted his head and blinked at the staff person. 'Tell Christophe it was amazing. I want his recipe for the watermelon relish.' Sam made a chef's kiss gesture then walked out into the carpark without a misstep in his stride. If Mick hadn't known Sam was a bit tipsy, he wouldn't have guessed from the way he walked.

'Thanks again.' Mick nodded and raced after Sam, who had stopped in the middle of the carpark and appeared to be lost. 'My car is this way.' He tucked his hand under Sam's elbow and walked him towards his car. After unlocking it, he opened the passenger door.

'Shouldn't you get in on the other side, if you are driving? Can you drive?'

'Yes, Sam, I'm sober and I'm driving. I'm also being polite to my date and opening the door.'

Sam smiled. 'Hmm. Weird but nice. Thanks.' Somehow Sam managed to look like all his bones were liquid as he sat down in the car. Mick checked that the door was clear and Sam wouldn't get hurt before he shut it and walked around to the driver's seat. As he sat down, he heard a gentle snore and glanced over to see Sam already asleep. He reached over and fastened Sam's seatbelt, before doing his own, and then turned the key. It would be a quiet drive back to Sam's farm.

***

Sam woke up with a raspy thump in the back of his head. He never got sick, what the hell? Oh, crap. He remembered—he'd had the matching wines with dinner last night, and he had only vague memories of the last couple of courses at the dinner. Hopefully he hadn't embarrassed himself. He really needed to stop being so impulsive; he was such a lightweight when it came to alcohol, hardly ever drinking more than one beer or two on an occasional quiet evening overlooking the farm. All that wine was a vastly different prospect; no wonder his head ached as if being crushed by the Kraken. He cracked one eye open—at least he was at home—but how had he gotten here?

'Coffee?' Mick stood in the doorway to his room, leaning on the frame like some sort of athletic god. The healthy alertness in his gaze only added to Sam's sense of being out of sorts.

'Yeah. Did we?' Sam had to know if they'd had sex. Mostly because he'd be super annoyed if he'd not remembered it.

'No. You slept in the car all the way here, and then fell asleep again as soon as you hit the bed.'

Sam frowned. 'That didn't answer the question.'

'True. No sex, because you weren't able to consent. I slept on the couch in the lounge. You can verify with your brother if you wish.'

'Nah, it's cool.' It wasn't—his head hurt like something awful—but at least his memory wasn't missing any crucial details. 'I believe you.'

Mick nodded. 'So ... coffee?'

'I think I'll have a shower first, and then, yeah, coffee. Thanks.' Sam dragged his heavy legs out of bed and made his way to the bathroom. Mick's eyes widened as he brushed past him, and weirdly all Sam's skin felt like it'd been torched. It wasn't until he got into the bathroom and caught sight of himself in the mirror—hell, he looked like shit—that he realised he was only wearing his undies. Had Mick undressed him? Whatever. So much for having a nice dinner with

Mick and confessing that he was ready to kiss him. It was obvious he wasn't ready for anything. He turned on the water and stepped underneath, even though the hot water hadn't warmed up yet. The fresh cold water was a slap to his skin, and shocked away some of his hangover. Damn, he was such a mess. When was he ever going to grow up and stop sabotaging his own life? The water suddenly heated up and he scrambled to turn on the cold tap to ensure he didn't burn himself. He shivered as the water temperature finally ended up at the decent level. He'd been an adult for nearly a decade and he still couldn't work out the basics of life and love. This wasn't something he could dismiss by saying adulthood was overrated. Life wasn't a silly meme. Sam kept his eyes closed and let the shower stream over him until the hot water ran out and it started to go cold again. He turned off the taps and gulped at the wave of guilt. They were in a drought; he shouldn't be wasting water like this just because he'd been foolish enough to drink too much last night. The concept of drying himself seemed beyond him; if he stepped out of the shower and got dressed, he'd have to talk to Mick and confront his feelings for him. Well, there was no time like the present. He may as well get it done with, and then he could go back to a lonely existence. With a cringe, he realised that he might have to quit SDH and find a new game to play.

Ten minutes later, with clean clothes on and teeth freshly brushed—a simple act that made him feel a thousand times better—Sam walked into the kitchen with his head held falsely high. The rich smell of coffee filled his nostrils and he almost forgot what he'd planned to say. Something about how he was too much of a mess to be anyone's partner, or some other blather like that. He rubbed the back of his neck.

'Here, have this.' Mick passed him a mug of instant coffee; nothing fancy for them out here on the farm. Caffeine was the key to instant coffee, not taste, and Sam inhaled deeply.

'Thank you. And thank you for bringing me home last night. I hope I wasn't too embarrassing.'

'No. Unless you count snuggling against me while I was paying the bill, you were delightful.'

'Really?' Sam's memory was starting to return, and he kept getting snippets of himself waving his cutlery around while talking enthusiastically about SDH strategy and underwater photography. Had he completely dominated the discussion with his hobbies? How dull and self-centred of him.

'Yes, really. You were a bit tipsy, that's all. And you seemed to be really enjoying the meal.'

Sam took a half-step backwards. 'By enjoying, do you mean, I was loud and obnoxious?'

'No.' Mick shook his head and grinned. 'I don't think you are capable of being obnoxious. You were cute and adorable, and I just wanted to kiss you and take you home forever.'

Sam's skin heated. 'You wanted to kiss me? But?'

'I still do. I think it's pretty obvious. I really like you, Sam. You could never embarrass me.'

Sam blinked at Mick, unable to make sense of his words. That couldn't be true. 'But I'm such a mess!'

'A delightful mess. Please don't change.'

Sam wished his head wasn't pounding quite so much, so he sipped his coffee and tried to process what Mick was saying. 'But I'm too impulsive?'

'It's not a character fault to be impulsive. You take chances, and yeah, sometimes they don't pay off, but sometimes they will. Everyone is a bit messy, and we all are unfinished products. I know I still have much learning to do—'

'You do? But you seem to be so, I don't know, like in charge of your life.'

Mick coughed. 'My mother says that we all make mistakes; it's how we fix them that matters.'

A glow, like hope, grew in Sam's belly, spreading through his limbs slowly. 'I don't think wine agrees with me. I'm more of a beer person.' It was a nonsensical thing to say, and yet he couldn't manage to say anything else. He really shouldn't have chosen the matching wines last night—he remembered why he had. The oysters, especially that watermelon relish, had been amazing, and when Celia had offered the wines to match the tasting plates, he'd only been thinking with his palate. 'Celia upsold me.'

'We all make mistakes.' Mick smiled, and it suddenly seemed like the whole world would be alright. 'I want you to know that being with you is not a mistake for me. I'm here ... deliberately ... because I want to be with you as more than friends. All of you, the messy parts, the cute drunk, the strategic brain behind Crassostrea, and the dorky aquaculturist who swims with sharks. Everything. I'm here for you.'

Sam couldn't speak, only nod. Aside from Kiet, no one had ever embraced all of him like that, and he really wished he wasn't fighting a vague hangover. Although the imperfectness of the moment made it bloody perfect. He put his half-drunk mug of coffee carefully on the table and walked towards Mick.

'Kiss me. I know I have a hangover and coffee breath—' Sam paused for a second.

'Actually, no, I brushed my teeth so it won't be too bad, plus, damn it, you're right. I'm a mess and I'm yours.'

'You can be my mess if you let me be your mess.' Mick leaned forward and touched his lips against Sam's mouth. Mick tasted like fresh coffee, and Sam sighed against his mouth. Everything about this was wrong. A first kiss when hungover, while standing awkwardly in the kitchen of the cottage he grew up in. But it was so right as well. The brush of stubble at the edges of Mick's lips. The hesitant touch from both of them, as if neither could believe this was actually happening. They'd been just friends for so long and finally, finally, Sam was kissing Mick.

'You taste just fine.' Mick's breath was warm, only a hair's breadth away from Sam's mouth.

'Like the first sip of a hot coffee on a freezing cold morning.'

Mick grinned. 'Welcoming and warming. Yeah.' He wrapped his arms around Sam's shoulders, pushed one hand up his neck and spread his fingers wide on Sam's skull. 'Now stop talking and kiss me again.'

Sam hummed an agreement and kissed Mick. This was where Sam wanted to be. In Mick's arms, being thoroughly kissed until his hangover faded and desire raced in his veins. Sam had been kissed plenty of times in his life, but never like this. Light and free, hot and needy, and he had to fight the instinct to tense up. But this was Mick and his body felt exactly right against Sam's. He placed his hands on Mick's shoulder blades. Mick rested his head against Sam's shoulder; being slightly shorter than Sam meant his head was the perfect height to nestle into the nook of his neck. Mick brushed his lips against Sam's neck, sending a flush over his skin. Everything changed from warm and new into something hotter, like he'd put cold hands into a sink of hot water, with prickles of heat swarming up his arms and over his skin. A good sensation, if slightly uncomfortable. 'More?' His voice cracked slightly.

'Yes, Sam. More. I don't think I'm the only one who feels this way.' Mick slid his hands down to Sam's waist with his hands, and paused, holding him tight.

'You aren't alone in wanting more.'

Mick slipped his hands slightly lower, so they rested against Sam's hips. Sam lifted his chin, brushing against Mick's hair, and breathed in sharply at the increased heat. One small movement, and Mick's thumbs might just brush his cock. Did he want that? Yes. Very much.

'Do you need more time?'

Sam nodded, and a stabbing pain reminded him of his hangover, then stilled as Mick moved his hands up Sam's side and gently traced the bottom of his ribs.

'I do. Want. More. Time.' Each word puffed out on its own breath of air, and with each word, Mick's strokes grew firmer until Sam said 'time' and Mick withdrew his hands and crossed them over his chest.

'I can wait. I get the sense you will be worth the wait.' If there was anything Mick could have said that made Sam decide to stop waiting, that was it. He swallowed. 'Ever since we met on SDH, you've been a good friend, and I don't want to mess that up by taking advantage of you.' Mick's voice washed away all the nasty tension that had built up and Sam cupped Mick's cheeks. *Oh.*

'Thank you.' Sam kissed Mick lightly on the mouth then pulled away. In that instant he knew he wanted Mick more than he'd ever wanted anyone; and he also knew he absolutely needed to wait. He extracted himself from the hug and stepped away. Mick lifted his fingers and held them to his lips. Good—he wasn't alone in feeling that brief kiss all the way down to his toes.

'Nothing like a kiss to get rid of a hangover.' From the way Mick's expression fell, Sam knew his joke was too much, but the thrill of desire head-butted against his hangover and when combined with the kiss, it was all too much.

'I'm sorry. I don't know why I said that.' Sam cringed and picked up his coffee to hide the way his heart was thumping unsteadily. He held the mug in front of him, as if it could shield Mick's view of his chest. 'Thank you for dinner. I had a wonderful time, and thank you for bringing me home safely. I'd better gulp this down and go down to the shed for work.'

'And thus, I'm effectively dismissed.'

Sam closed his eyes. 'That's not what I mean. This—' he waved his coffee mug and some splashed over the side, splatting on the wooden floor of the cottage '—is a bit intense and I...'

'Need time to figure it out. I know.' Mick sounded so disappointed, Sam's chest felt like it might cave in.

'Damn it. Come here.' He put down the coffee and reached out for Mick before he could rush off. 'You scare me and yet I want you so much.'

'I understand.'

'You do?' Sam leaned his cheek against Mick, revelling in the rough stubble against his own face.

'Yes. Take your time. I'm not offended by your process.'

Sam shifted so he could stare at Mick. 'My process? All I'm doing is grappling with a little lust. I don't want to ruin our good friendship.'

'Which is admirable. Look, I'm going to head off and leave you to figure it out. When you do, send me a DM or something and I'll drop by.' Mick smiled. 'It really is okay. Stop overthinking. I don't mind waiting for you.'

Sam nodded and pressed a quick kiss to Mick's lips. 'Thank you.'

Chapter 11

The next two weeks passed in delirious happiness, and Sam had to fight the urge to stress about life being too good to be true. Every few days, Mick had turned up at the farm, either before or after his shift, and they'd played SDH together with Mick on his laptop and Sam on his computer. They'd laughed, chatted and, yes, kissed. Today, Sam was ready to go further. Tonight, he was going to invite Mick to stay the night. Kiet and Zoe had gone down to Sydney for a few days to see clients. Sam's leg jiggled as he waited for Mick to drop by on his way home from work. The second he heard the crunch of car tyres on the gravel outside the cottage, he leaped off his chair. Sam bolted through the house, flung open the back door, and reminded himself to take a breath. He slowed his steps, then leaned casually against one of the posts holding up the porch roof.

'Hello.' Mick stepped out of his car, shut the door, and walked towards the cottage. 'Have a good day?'

'Yes, and you?'

'Yeah, same old. I brought some fresh bread from town. Can't have you making everything for dinner.'

Sam grinned and jumped off the porch and walked the few strides to meet Mick. Mick touched him on the shoulder and leaned in for a brief kiss.

'Come in. I have some prawns and steak for a barbecue, but there's no rush for dinner.' Sam's babbling was ended in the best way as Mick kissed him again. The rush of desire licked like flames up his spine, heating his veins, and he stamped down the need to grab Mick by the hand and drag him into his bedroom. He lifted his head, breaking the kiss, so he could get some air into his lungs and slow down his galloping heartbeat.

'I'd like that.'

Sam blinked a couple of times. Oh, Mick meant the food, not the whole bedroom thing. He might be a glorious kisser, but he probably wasn't a mind-reader.

'My brother's away for a few days for work.'

'You mentioned that already when you invited me around for dinner.'

Sam's cheeks warmed. 'Yes, I did. Come in.'

Mick kissed him once more, then walked into the house with a little wriggle of his backside as he went up the stairs. A rush of heat bloomed on Sam's face and he lifted his chin to the sky to let the evening summer sun glow on his skin instead. Then he might have some sort of excuse for the flush on his cheeks.

'You tease.' Sam laughed as he watched Mick place his shopping on the bench. A loaf of bread, and a couple of nice beers from the local brewery. For the past few weeks, they'd flirted at every chance they could, light happy moments that filled Sam with a gleeful joy.

Mick tilted his head to one side. 'I'm glad you decided to take slow steps with us. I didn't realise I needed that. Back in Sydney, I ... Well, a few things happened that knocked my sense of self around, and I didn't realise how much they'd affected me until I came here.'

'And I thought we were just gaming together.' Sam tried to keep the mood light, even though he really wanted Mick to open up about his past. The few times he'd tried to pry, Mick had closed him down and moved the conversation back to SDH—just like Sam had done now, thinking he may as well do it first before he felt disappointed.

'Is that what you call it?'

'Yeah. Now stop fussing with that food and come and kiss me.'

Mick paused. 'What about your brother? Aren't you worried he'll walk in?'

Sam grinned. 'He's already left. We have the house to ourselves.' His chest rose and fell faster than normal and his shirt was tight against his skin. He really wanted to get naked with Mick; no, more than that. He wanted to touch Mick, see his skin, it was more than just the nakedness. Sam wanted to be closer to Mick, against him in a tight hug, wrapped around him. He wanted everything.

'I mean, you saw me naked after we went to dinner that time, and I haven't...' He stopped before he said more. He'd already revealed too much of his desire. They'd agreed on slow, and here was Sam once more leaping in first.

'Well, then, in the interests of fairness.' Mick untucked his shirt, and slowly pulled it up to reveal a dark line of hair that disappeared into his jeans. Strong abs shifted as he lifted his arms and tugged the shirt over his head. Sam was a little woozy at the sight of all that naked flesh. The pecs, the biceps, the slight tremble at the bottom of Mick's throat. Sam's mouth watered.

'I can't believe you've been hiding that from me.' Sam closed the gap between them, grabbed Mick's shirt, and flung it onto the couch. He stroked his hands over Mick's bare chest, fingers trailing through the thick carpet of hair, across the broad, strong muscles, until Mick let out a low rumble of a groan.

'More?' Sam asked and Mick answered with a desperate open-mouthed kiss. Their tongues stroked each other, needy with a strong push and pull of desire between them. Sam's lungs burned for air, but he still wanted more. More of Mick's heady taste. He ran his hands up to Mick's shoulders, and then down his muscular arms to his elbows. Mick placed his hands on Sam's waist and Sam stepped even closer, pressing his erection against Mick. The resulting groan was incredible, searing him with another lick of desire that inflamed his blood, most of which had headed south. Sam glided his hands back up Mick's arms, and across his shoulders. He'd done this many times before over the past few weeks, but never before with his bare hands on Mick's naked skin. Sam stroked one hand up the back of Mick's neck, gripping him tighter as they deepened their kiss, and with the other, he glided his palm over Mick's shoulder blade. The texture of Mick's skin changed, with ridges of scar tissue across his back.

'Stop, please.' Mick flinched away from Sam and he stepped back with his hands held up in the air.

'Of course. I'm sorry.'

'I can't do this.'

'Can't do what?' The sudden change became a cool chill in the air.

'This.' Mick waved his arms around helplessly, the motion reflected in the gritty tone of his voice.

'It's just a scar. I'm not bothered by it.'

Mick closed his eyes and Sam cursed under his breath.

'Do you want your shirt?' Sam asked. Perhaps doing something practical would help ease the tension in between them. The room shimmered with unspoken strain, as if they'd both cut their fingers while making salad and now didn't know what to do.

'I'll get it.' Mick turned to grab his shirt, and Sam pinched his lips together so he wouldn't gasp at the sight of Mick's back. Long scars ran down his left side, from the base of his neck, across his shoulder blade, and almost all the way down to the waistband of his jeans. They were red and puckered and lumpy, like the skin had been ripped off and badly patched back on.

'I really don't care about your scars. I like you, Mick. All of you.'

Mick spun around. 'I care very much about my scars. Don't tell me you don't care.'

'Okay?'

'I earned these scars. I won't have them dismissed as unimportant.' Mick's face was red and blotchy and his eyes narrowed. 'I won't.'

'Okay. I understand.'

'You can never understand.' Mick shoved his shirt over his head, pulling it down over his face with vigour.

'I can try. Please let me try.'

'No. Keep the bread.' Mick marched out of the house, slamming the door of the cottage so the whole bloody house shuddered. Sam didn't have to wait long to hear Mick's car start up. Gravel crunched as Mick drove away.

What the heck had just happened? Sam collapsed onto the couch, resting his head on the back, and stared up at the peeling paint on the ceiling. They really ought to do some maintenance before the bloody cottage fell down around them. He closed his eyes and tried to think back through the conversation. Mick had been as keen as he was, he'd kissed him with everything, and then when Sam had touched his scar, he'd flinched as if Sam had punched him in the nose. The complete change of pace left Sam with a kind of whiplash. He'd tried to console Mick and that had made it worse. He jumped to his feet and paced back and forth, but action didn't help either.

'I'm going for a run,' he announced, then slapped himself on the forehead. Kiet and Zoe were away; he didn't need to tell them where he was going when he was the only damned person in the cottage. Sam paced down the hallway, threw open the back door and stepped outside where he shook out his boots and slipped them on. The red rear lights of Mick's car disappeared around the end of the hill.

Sam jumped off the porch and started jogging away towards the last vestiges of the sunset, away from the farm, away from the cove. His work boots weren't really designed for running, but they'd do. He needed the pounding jar of each stride more than he cared about the blisters he'd have tomorrow. Sam turned down the driveway, past the missing gum tree that had fallen in a storm on Christmas Day, and kept running. What had actually happened? What was Mick hiding from Sam? The scars obviously meant something to Mick, because otherwise he wouldn't have reacted with such force. But what?

It wasn't until he'd run all the way to the end of the road that his lungs began to burn, each breath sucking in desperately for oxygen. Sam stopped and stared out at the black ocean with the reflection of the stars above bouncing shards of light off the waves. The sun had disappeared behind the hill, leaving the water dark.

Even after all the months chatting to Mick online, Mick didn't trust him with the story of his scars. What had actually happened? What was Mick hiding from Sam? And why would he assume that Sam didn't care about him? Obviously, something bad had happened to him. If Sam hadn't let himself get overwhelmed by Mick's incredible body, his cinnamon and fresh grass scent overlaid with the antiseptic of his job, and his gorgeous brown eyes, perhaps they could've had a proper conversation about it. Sam cared for Mick—surely that was obvious. And Sam had no clue how to talk to Mick about this, while Mick wasn't being honest with him.

Slowly, Sam turned back to the road, and walked all the way home. Alone to an empty cottage.

Chapter 12

Mick woke up slowly, and a little disoriented, with his phone alarm blaring at him. He punched the screen with his finger to turn the racket off. His jeans were too tight, rubbing against his hips and legs in a way that made him want to rip them off. His skin was a bit sticky with humidity. The dry, hot January air had turned moist overnight as tropical thunderstorms pretended to be monsoonal without the huge dumping of rain. The cycle of thunderstorms in the evening, then bright hot days, meant the humidity was thick like molasses with the air almost dripping until the water fell as rain at night, then evaporated all day to repeat the cycle endlessly. Blaming the weather didn't help.

For the third night in a row, Mick had fallen asleep on his couch, still wearing his clothes after spending too long distracting himself from the heavy weight on his shoulders. He should never had taken off his shirt in front of Sam. He didn't know what had led to that moment.

Yes, he did. He needed to stop lying to himself. The best kisses ever had led to that moment. He couldn't resist Sam, and he'd pushed him away before Sam had the chance to reject him, like Xavier had after the factory fire. Xavier hadn't even waited until Mick was out of hospital before he'd left. The message was still saved on his phone.

Xavier: I'm not coming back. I need someone who is good for my image.

Mick's ears roared and his veins pulsed with the usual flood of angry heat that surged whenever he read that. As if his scarred back would ever be seen by anyone else when he was in public with Xavier. He could still be good for Xavier, he was still the same Mick, still handsome enough to stand beside Xavier. No. That way of thinking wasn't helpful. Like his new therapist, Maddie, said: he didn't need to be good for someone else. He couldn't let someone else define whether he was worthy. He was already good enough for himself.

Mick should probably delete Xavier's message and work out how to move on. For far too long, Mick had forgiven Xavier for not being there for him after the accident, for cheating on him over and over, for basically being abusive. Just because the violence was verbal didn't make it less hurtful. He'd convinced himself that Xavier's apologies were the only real parts of their relationship; that he truly didn't mean it when he was too rough in bed, and that Xavier needed to cheat because Mick couldn't give him enough. Mick's scars were a symbol of how pathetic he'd been. Even after leaving hospital, he'd begged Xavier to come back. Looking back, he couldn't believe he'd done that. He had loving parents. He didn't need Xavier. And he didn't need Sam either. Mick didn't need anyone. He peeled off his jeans and started to walk towards his bathroom for a shower. Time to go to work and do the one thing he was good at: helping people who were hurt. Mick nearly tripped on that annoying edge of the rug in his lounge, imagining Sam's laugh ringing snarkily in his head.

'Yes, I see the irony in helping others when I won't let myself be helped. I'm going to see a therapist, you dickhead.' Now Mick was talking to himself. Shit. Sam had seen his scars and he hadn't cared about them. He might have dismissed all the hurt that Mick associated with his scars, but he had touched them as if they were any other part of him. Like his elbow, or foot. Mick leaned his head against the wall of his hallway. He'd pushed Sam away just when he'd given him a gift—acceptance. Sam's gift mattered, and now Mick needed to apologise.

***

Three days after the moment Sam labelled 'the argument'—even though it wasn't really one because Mick hadn't argued, just scarpered away, leaving Sam alone with too many questions—Kiet and Zoe returned home. Having them home helped Sam get out of his own head. For those three days, he'd spent too much time on the internet, playing games that weren't SDH, or chatting to his cousins and pretending life was just fine. Last night he'd stayed up late chatting to Kiet about Nok again, and together they'd found a way of dealing with her disappearance. Maybe they would never know what happened, but they had each other and it would have to be enough.

Sam opened one eye as sharp light infiltrated his thin curtains. He pulled them back and the dawn shone inside like a typical late January day. He'd slept in. Blast. The light was bright with the faint smell of bushfire smoke in the air. Sam opened the Rural Fire Service app on his phone and leaped out of bed with a gasp. His whole body snapped to attention.

'Kiet!' Sam yelled while trying to keep his pulse slow. A fire was burning only thirty kilometres away. It wasn't close enough to be a threat to their cottage or sheds, and was only at *Watch and Act*, not *Emergency*, level, but it wasn't the fire itself that was the problem. Sam needed to monitor the water conditions. If they got too much ash runoff in the river it would ruin the oysters. Thirty kilometres was too close, especially this close to the river's edge. It'd take him ages to get there on the river in his tinny, although he could hoon for the most part until he got to the resort and the river narrowed.

His brother's groan emanated through his bedroom door.

'Kiet, there's a fire about thirty clicks inland on the river.'

'How bad?' Kiet grumbled.

Sam leaned his forehead against the door. 'Watch and Act. Check the app; looks like it's at the river's edge.' Thankfully it was on the headland side of the river, away from the town, so no threat to Marandowie or Rainbow Cove—though there were a few scattered houses on that side of the river. The headland was hard to access by road, with the main crossing quite far inland where the river narrowed down, and most of it was bush and his mate Eddie's farm. Oh crap. Eddie and Celia's mum was sick. Sam needed to go and help them. He sucked in a deep breath, and his lungs twinged with the acidic smoke in the air. He didn't need to panic. Eddie was a volunteer firefighter, he'd be prepared. Kiet groaned and a curse rumbled through the door.

'I don't want to remove all our crops from the river, either.' Sam didn't dread the work, only the implications of it. 'At this stage, we'll just monitor and maybe pull all the spat out and put them back into the seeding shed.'

'I'll be there soon.'

'Okay.' Sam jogged the few strides back to his room and dragged on some clothes. Half of their friends were volunteers for the local fire brigade, so they'd already be out of bed and helping put it out. It must have started with lightning, and the bloody bush was tinder-dry at the moment. It wouldn't take much. So much for being stressed about whether he wanted to do anything about Mick and his angry response to Sam touching his scars. Their entire business, their livelihood, was at risk. A gut-wrenching anxiety swept through his veins, chilly on this hot day. The river might not be impure today, but the water clarity tests would soon let him know how urgent the problem was. With a few more breaths, Sam realised he had several days to work this out. He didn't need to panic or do anything impulsive. The last time they'd had a massive issue was several years ago when there were bad floods more than three hundred kilometres inland and the dirty muddy water had taken a few days to get to the farm. They'd salvaged most of their crop and the losses hadn't been too bad. He'd have time to prepare; at least once he knew the extent of the problem. Water tests first, then he'd drive one of the boats up the river to do a visual assessment of the fire.

Several hours later, Sam's back ached after helping Kiet remove all their spat trays from the river as a precaution. The older oysters closer to harvesting size would be alright for the moment, as would the mid-sized ones that wouldn't be harvested until next year. They'd have to be; there wasn't space in the seeding shed for them. It was always the risk. Poor water quality would take out at least one year's worth of crops because they could harvest this year's crop—selling it for canning, rather than fresh, at a lower profit margin—and they could protect the babies in the shed, but the mid-sized ones would have to cope with the water quality. On the upside, they were the ones that had time to filter all the awful water out, assuming the water quality improved again. If the water got bad enough—even for a week or so—many of the oysters left in that water would suffocate and die. Their boat had a crane on it to assist them as they lifted the spat trays from the river, but there was still a lot of physical work in stacking them on the boat, then restacking them on the jetty before using the forklift to move them into the seeding shed where filtered water would keep them alive and healthy. It took several boatloads and a whole morning's work to get them all safely back in the seeding shed. These babies were most at risk when water quality reduced.

'Hey Zoe, you're getting really good at driving the forklift.' Sam clapped her on the back. 'Thanks for the help.'

'It's no problem. I'd much rather do the accounts, but you know, I'm starting to enjoy this farming life.'

Kiet slung his arm around her waist. 'So she says after only a month living here. Wait till winter when it's all cold and wet and miserable.'

'I'll have you to keep me warm.' She smiled up at Kiet and Sam rolled his eyes.

'You two lovebirds!'

Kiet winked. 'I had to put up with it when you were with Lizzy.'

Sam grinned, even though he didn't feel at all like it; the expression was designed to keep away the tension between them. 'Now that she's not the thief, you've decided to call her Lizzy. Nice.'

'I'm sorry for all of that. The timing made her look guilty.'

'I appreciate that, and that you were trying to protect me and the farm, but it'd be good if you trusted my judgement too.' Sam loved Kiet with all his heart, he was the best brother, but at times, he still seemed to think Sam was the

naïve sixteen-year-old who needed his protection.
No wonder it stung when Lizzy used the same
reason for breaking up with him. At least Mick
hadn't said he was too young to understand. His
chest squeezed tight—he'd hurt Mick by touching
him—and he yearned to reach out and say sorry.
He hadn't known about the scars or that Mick
would hate being touched. Something stopped
him though, a twinge in his gut that told him to
give Mick a bit of space.

'You're right. I should have. I needed
someone to blame because I'd let it go on for
too long, and Lizzy was right there as an obvious
target.'

Zoe beckoned to Sam. 'Come here. Bring it
in for a family hug. Both of you need to stop
blaming each other and yourselves and put the
blame squarely with Andersen. He stole from
you. He chose to be toxic, he's been caught,
and he's going to suffer the consequences of
everything he's done. We are a team.'

Sam stepped towards her and let her drag
him in for a hug with her and Kiet. After a
moment, he pulled away. He needed to check
the water quality and see if his friend Eddie was
okay.

'I'm going up the river to have a look at the
fire and see how bad it is. Be back in a couple
of hours.' He stepped off the jetty into one of

the smaller, more nimble boats, and started the engine with a roar and a puff of two-stroke smoke.

'That's the way. Go for a cruise and leave us to do all the hard work.' Kiet's laughter followed him across the water, and he waved casually at the two of them as he steered the boat up the river.

It was a gorgeous day with a hot wind pushing him along as he increased the throttle and raced towards the fire zone. The boat quickly stopped slapping on the waves and began to ride high in the water, increasing in speed. He guided it along the main channel until he passed the poles outside the Rainbow Cove Resort that indicated the shallow parts of the riverbed, and he squinted at the glare off the water. Even through sunglasses, the light was sharp, especially now it was nearly midday. As the river narrowed, Sam listened carefully to the motor and kept his eye on the variable current of the different parts of the river as it bent and twisted around. It'd been a while since he'd driven up here and the lack of water depth in the river—damned drought—meant he needed to be careful to make sure he didn't bottom out at any point. The wind blew from behind him, pushing him north, so he made good time to the location of the fire, and the smell of smoke still wasn't very strong because it was blowing away from him. He rounded a bend in the river and cut back on the throttle when he saw that the bush ahead of him was smouldering with blackened trunks. It must have been burning for a while, or moving quickly, as there were no active flames here, just embers on the ground and trees, and he realised it was the wind direction that had prevented him from smelling the smoke much earlier. He didn't check the app every day, so it might have been burning for a while already.

Sam slowed up the boat and kept to the far side of the river as he drove past the fire. Around the next bend, Sam caught sight of flames, licking at the tall trees, and the heat from the land intensified. He probably should turn around and head back to the farm before this heat became too much. Hold on. Was that a flashing light he could see? He crouched lower in the boat and sped up a little, casting his gaze back and forth over the water for a safe pathway. With the glare of the fire bouncing off the water, it was becoming impossible to read the river for current and depth.

Sam guided the boat around a bend in the river. He gasped, then coughed as the hot air hit his lungs, and he grabbed a grubby cloth from the side of the boat to cover his mouth.

Mick stood in the middle of the river holding another man in his arms. On the bank of the river, an ambulance was parked sideways at the top of the concrete boat ramp, and another paramedic—Sam recognised Leila—stood beside the ambulance with a fire extinguisher.

Chapter 13

'Sam. Oh my God. Thank you.' Mick had no idea what had made Sam drive his boat up the river, but he nearly collapsed with gratitude. The only thing stopping his knees from giving out was the need to keep Bert's broken leg out of the water. The injured firefighter was fucking heavy, even with the river helping hold some of his weight. The smoke stung like acid in his throat and he struggled for each breath, hauling in more smoke, more heat, with every inhalation. Even with a face mask on, it hadn't really helped, just cut down some of the smoke, but it was the heat that sucked all his energy away. Adrenaline spiked, making his heart race, and his muscles tremble and burn with lactic acid. It didn't matter, he wasn't going to let Bert's leg get wet. He'd stand here all night if he had to. Until Sam arrived, Mick honestly thought he would die as fire raged around him. The intense heat reminded him of the factory fire, and past images flashed through his brain.

'Get in.' Sam jumped out of the boat. River water splashed over Mick's back, a cool relief. 'There's not much time.'

'Can you fit Bert in that boat? He needs to get out of here quickly, and obviously...' Mick nodded at the raging fire behind him. There was no way he'd be able to drive the ambulance up the driveway to safety, not with flames leaping between the canopy of the gum trees on either side of the path. The intense heat made it hard to breathe. A slight wind change would bring the fire closer to them; so far only Leila and good luck were keeping the fire from burning the ambulance. No one wanted to get caught in an ember attack, and from the way the flames danced in the trees just over there, Sam was right. There wasn't much time.

Sam glanced over at Leila. 'I have room for everyone. It'll be a squash, but I'm not leaving any of you here. Not with the way that fire is raging.'

'Okay. Help me with Bert. Stay away from his leg and try to keep it dry.' Bert was high on painkillers, so he probably wouldn't notice being jostled. The break was a bad one, an open wound with bone visible through the pants of his fire uniform. If he got river water in that wound, it would get infected and he might lose the leg. Mick wasn't going to let that happen, not on his watch. Mick had trussed it in a temporary splint, and with Leila's help, they'd covered the splinted leg in plastic wrap. It wasn't waterproof enough to survive being dunked in the river, but it would keep most of the smoke and a few splashes off the wound. They'd just managed to finish before the fire came too close and Mick had had to flee into the river for safety. There was a small clearing by the top of the boat ramp where he'd parked the ambulance. Leila was fighting a losing battle trying to keep the flames away from the vehicle.

'Leila!' he called out, coughing as his throat filled with smoky grit.

'Come. Forget the ambulance.' Sam spoke for him, and a rush of gratitude added a welcome coolness to Mick's overheated, overworked veins.

She splashed into the river. 'What do you need?'

'Hold the side of the boat. I'll hold the other side, then we'll be able to keep it stable while Mick lifts Bert into it.' Sam pointed to the front of the boat as he moved to the far side. Sweat streamed down Mick's face and back with each step, leaving a salty taste in his mouth. His legs were like jelly and his arm muscles screamed as he lifted Bert's weight out of the water. Sam lifted the far side of the boat so the edge near Mick was lower, meaning he didn't have to hoist Bert so high.

'Put him with his back at the front of the boat, so he's facing the rear of the boat. The leg will be most stable in the middle of the boat.'

'Okay.' Mick's lungs screamed. Trying to speak and lift while the fire sucked away all the oxygen turned his voice into a hoarse whisper. Bert landed on the seat with a guttural groan. Sam grabbed the fishing tackle box from underneath the seat Bert was on.

'Here, this might be useful to prop under his leg.'

'Thanks.'

Sam nodded and waved to Leila. 'Your turn. Rest your stomach on the edge of the boat, then swing your legs in sideways.' Sam's instructions reminded Mick of the first day they'd gone snorkelling at Sam's farm. He'd taught Mick the same technique, and the memory was a joyful respite. It pushed away the rampaging factory fire imagery in his head. The dry heat from the fire intensified. It evaporated the sweat off his face before he had the chance to wipe it off. It was so hard to breath, and his feet felt like bricks on the end of his legs, as if he'd run a marathon, not stood still for a while in a river.

'Mick. Get in. The two of you need to sit either there or there.' Sam pointed to two spots, and Mick swung into the boat using the same method. Leila sat beside Bert at the front of the boat, before he took the spot next to Bert's leg. Sam turned the boat around, facing them along the river.

'Do you need anything from the ambulance?' Sam asked. The radio would be good, but as Mick glanced at the vehicle, flames flicked along the dirt.

'Too late. Let's get Bert to safety.'

Sam jumped into the seat next to the engine. Bert groaned as the boat lurched with Sam's weight.

'Sorry.' Sam lowered the engine into the water and pulled the cable to start it up. The buzzing roar of the engine should have been loud, but the fire roared louder. 'Hey Mick. Can you sit here and balance the boat up a bit?' Sam yelled as he patted the seat next to him, then held out his arm, so Mick could shift away from his spot on the floor next to Bert's foot and onto the seat. Mick gripped Sam's forearm and sat facing towards Bert and the front of the boat. Now they were on their way, hopefully to safety, Mick had time to think back over the incident to figure out what had gone wrong. They'd arrived on the scene and the rest of the fire crew had directed him to park near the edge of the river. They'd helped carry Bert into the back of the ambulance, then the fire truck had raced off up the driveway to try and stop the spread of the fire. They'd told him the driveway should work as a firebreak, but not to wait too long as the fire was moving quickly, and he should get out of there. They hadn't been wrong; he'd barely had time to give Bert some painkillers when the bush had roared with flame—an intense noise he'd never forget—and their path out had been cut off.

Leila had radioed through to describe the issue; the station had advised to stay by the river and use the water to keep safe from the fire if needed, to shelter in the river submerged under woollen blankets. She promised she'd keep them updated—crap, they hadn't told them about the boat—then they'd gone back to work.

'Mick?' Leila sounded flustered.

'Yes?'

She held up her hands and her palms were blistered and raw. She must have burned them on the fire extinguisher when she was trying to keep the fire away from the ambulance. Mick cast his view around the boat for anything he could use to help. A bucket tucked in the side would help.

'Sam? Do you have any plastic bags?'

'Maybe in the tackle box.'

Mick gently shifted Bert's foot and opened the tackle box. A couple of small plastic bags were in the bottom tray, and he tipped the contents out into the box. He lowered his mask and held them in his teeth as he placed Bert's leg down to rest. A rank fishy taste added to the smoke. He gritted his teeth as he grabbed the bucket. It was the work of seconds to hold it over the edge of the boat and fill it with river water. He put it on the floor of the boat, between Leila's legs and she used her legs to keep it steady.

'But the water isn't clean. I'll get an infection,' Leila protested.

'I know. Put these bags over your hands first. It's not perfect but it's better than nothing.' Mick turned the bags inside out and helped Leila cover her burned palms with the plastic and she dunked them in the bucket. After that, no one spoke as they traversed the river away from the fire. Mick ignored the way Sam's arm brushed against his with the motion of the boat. It was comforting having him here, close by, as they moved towards safety, although his heartrate stayed elevated. Understandable given the stressful circumstances, and he realised he was used to making that assessment on other people, not himself.

'There's a boat ramp a few bends from here on the western side of the river. If my phone has any reception, we can call someone to meet us there; or if not, we'll have to go most of the way to the boat ramp at the resort. There's a few other ramps, but they're all private access and who knows what condition the driveways will be in.' Sam leaned down and grabbed his phone from a drawer in the back of the boat beside the engine and cursed. Presumably he had no reception, and Mick turned his attention back to his patients. Leila started to look pale under her tanned olive skin. 'You okay, Leila?'

'It hurts and the boat...' She raised one of her hands up and covered her mouth. Mick automatically leaned towards her, moved her arm away from her mouth, and helped her lean over the side. The boat rocked dangerously.

'Hey, stay still or you'll tip us all in the river.'

Leila vomited over the side, covering herself and Mick with the pungent acidic spray of droplets as the wind carried the lighter chunks along. Mick was so glad he'd covered Bert's wound because this could have been catastrophic for him. The infection risk alone was enough to increase Mick's pulse rate to a dangerous level. The engine noise reduced, and the boat slowed. A towel slapped over his shoulder.

'Here you go. This might help.' Sam sounded unfussed by the whole drama, although Bert looked pretty green. He was high enough on morphine that it wouldn't surprise Mick if Bert's stomach also emptied out soon. Mick cleaned up Leila as much as he could, trying to keep the vomit away from her blistered hands.

The engine roared again, and the boat picked up speed. It took longer than Mick wanted before the river widened—he had to force his leg not to jiggle and upset Bert as he tried to wish the boat faster—and they pulled into the boat ramp at the Rainbow Cove Resort. An ambulance waited for them. Keerthi stood on the jetty waving at them.

'How did they know?'

'I texted Kiet to let him know we were on our way. I didn't have enough reception to call, but I hoped a text message would get through.' Sam navigated the way up the ramp, switched off the engine, and jumped out with a splash. The boat lurched forward a bit and Mick had to grab the side of the boat so he didn't slide off the seat and bump Bert. Before Mick could blink, Sam had tied the boat against the wooden jetty that ran down one side of the ramp. Mick clambered out onto the jetty.

'What happened?' Keerthi's voice was full of concern.

'We got trapped by fire. Had to leave the ambulance there.' He'd ended up in a bad situation, only to be saved by Sam's lucky presence. He quickly gave Keerthi and George, the other paramedic, a rundown of events. Together, all three helped move their patients into the back of the ambulance. Leila first, because she could move herself, then a more difficult movement to get Bert out of the boat safely. Sam stood on the far side of the boat, in the water, to help steady the boat as Mick stood at the back of the boat with legs spread wide to lift Bert up to Keerthi and George.

'You need to come too and get checked out. You don't look great,' Keerthi said to Mick.

'No. I'm fine. I need to get back to the station and see what else needs to be done.' Now that Keerthi had mentioned it, he knew there would be piles of paperwork to fill out and now they were less one truck.

'If you are sure, boss?' Keerthi's tone made him question whether he should, except...

'Absolutely. It's what you would do if you were me. Please, get Bert to the hospital quickly before infection gets into that break. We'll chat later.' Mick waved her away, and waited until the lights were on, and the ambulance drove away before he let out his breath.

'I'm sure Xander or Christophe can find someone to drive you into town if that's what you need. I need to take the boat home.' Sam still stood in ankle-deep water, looking up at Mick as he sat on the edge of the jetty with his feet still dangling in the boat. 'You look wrecked though. Maybe you should have a shower and a nap first.'

A shower and clean clothes sounded so good. Mick closed his eyes, imagining the cool stream of water washing the smoke off his skin, but then shook his head. He really needed to get back to work and let everyone know he was fine and figure out how to manage the station without one ambulance. 'Where?'

'At the resort. You remember we ate at Christophe's; besides, Zoe works for Xander, the owner. Everyone here is great; they'll find a spare room for you. Times like this, the whole community steps up and helps everyone.' Sam spoke as if it were true, and Mick realised his body was shaking a little with the vestiges of the adrenaline rush that'd been keeping him alert until now. He rolled himself up to stand on the jetty. Standing was harder than he expected, and his knees felt like bloody jelly. He must have been in more danger than he'd let his consciousness believe. Another image from the Sydney fire flashed, and he hung his head. He'd need more than a shower to deal with the aftermath of this. He automatically patted his scars and jerked his hand away when he realised what he'd done.

'Okay.'

Sam slipped back into the boat.

'Where are you going?'

'I can't leave the boat here.'

Mick's stomach sank. Now the rescue was done, the last thing he wanted to do was introduce himself to strangers and ask for help. He was the helper, he didn't get helped, and it always made him uncomfortable to reach out.

'Actually, you know what. I can. I'll just let the staff know I'll pick it up when I return Christophe's car. Let me come with you.' Sam fiddled with the boat a bit, giving Mick time to adjust to the sudden change of heart from Sam. Thank God he'd decided to stay. The rush of gratitude was stronger than he should feel in this particular moment, and he knew it was overlaid with his feelings for Sam. As much as he wanted to convince himself that he'd feel this grateful if anyone had offered him a chance to clean up before he went back to the office, he knew the feeling was bigger—almost overwhelming—because it was Sam offering help. He might have brushed away anyone else. Sam had literally saved his life. If he'd been lacking in oxygen during the fire, it had nothing on the realisation that he would never be with Sam. The parallel to his break-up with Xavier was too much: a fire resulting in Mick needing someone. He couldn't put himself through that agony again.

'Come this way.' Sam sloshed up the ramp, his arm pointing towards the impressive building clinging to the side of the hill. Mick had sat inside those big glass windows looking out, but it looked different from underneath. Imposing. A shiver ran down his spine and he shook out his hands. He needed to check in with the station and let someone know where he was. He was still on shift, after all. There was a chance Keerthi had phoned the whole situation through as she'd taken Bert to the hospital, but Mick wanted to confirm for himself. Besides, he had to do something practical or he was going to collapse.

'Can I borrow your phone?'

'Sure.' Sam held out the device. 'Hold on, let me unlock it for you.' He did that, then handed it over. Mick hesitated, suddenly unable to remember the staff number. Odd, he was usually good at that stuff. The number was stored in his own phone, which was still in the ambulance. He punched in Triple 0, pushing away the guilty reflex at taking up valuable emergency space.

'Police, ambulance, or fire?'

'Ambulance.' Mick followed up with his staff number and asked to be transferred to the correct person.

'Connecting you now.'

'Thanks.' He waited for the call to connect and then introduced himself to the staff member at the end of the line. They had already heard from Keerthi, much to his relief. 'I'm going to get cleaned up and will be back at the station in less than an hour.'

'Can you make it less? It's going to be all hands on deck for the rest of the day. This fire has gotten away on the fire crews. They've been ordered to withdraw.'

'I'll try my best.' Mick didn't need a shower. He'd head back to the station now. He finished the call, then handed the phone back to Sam. 'Hey, thanks. Don't worry about talking to your friends. I need to get back to the station.'

'Now?'

'Yes, now. I'm still on call, and with this fire, they are expecting more callouts. I have to be there.'

Sam nodded. 'Come this way. We'll borrow Christophe's car.' Sam paced up the hill and disappeared through a door in the side of the building. As Mick raced after him, he heard Sam's laugh. How could anyone laugh now?

'Mate, I know, but it's an emergency. I need to borrow your car...' Sam's voice was suddenly serious and Mick's tension ratcheted skywards. He didn't want to be in Sam's debt more than he already was. It was too close to the way Xavier had calculated what Mick owed him, and he couldn't do that again. It would break him. He had to end this now.

A French accent pierced the air, laden with sarcasm. 'Stop dripping on my clean floor. And why do you need to borrow my car?'

'Just because, mate. Are you so obsessed with your work that you didn't hear the ambo arrive?'

'An ambulance. Who is hurt?' The French accent now carried concerned tones. Mick leaned on the doorway for support and watched Sam chat with a broad-shouldered man in a chef's hat. They'd eaten here and he'd heard about Christophe without meeting him. No, he wasn't going to remember how that dinner was the most fun evening he'd ever had with anyone. The zero pressure enjoyment of watching Sam eat and drink and giggle. His chest clenched tight.

'A firey. I picked them up in my boat and met the ambo here. But I need to take one of them back to the station.'

'I see. Of course you can take my car and, here, have some bread too.'

Sam took the bread and the keys from the chef and turned around with a cheeky grin that seemed out of place given the drama of the day. 'Always with the bread. Christophe, this is my friend Mick. He's new to town, works as a paramedic.'

'Welcome. The ambulance left you behind?'

Mick tried to chuckle, but it came out as a strangled croak. 'Yeah, long story. They needed it more than me, I'm just the boss. Thank you for letting Sam borrow your car. I need to get back to the station.' The sooner he got back to work, the better. He couldn't deal with having to explain *why* he couldn't be with Sam. But he knew he had to end it. Just cut the relationship off. Delete his SDH account. Move to a new town. Yes, it was drastic, but that's what he needed to do. A dramatic solution to a large problem. He couldn't be in love with someone who'd rescued him; he couldn't owe Sam. He couldn't live with a debt waiting to be paid.

'It's no problem. Please have some bread too. You look like you need a good feed.' Christophe picked up a lethal-looking knife and turned towards the bench, so his actions were hidden from Mick—not on purpose, just by the broad width of Christophe's back.

'Christophe. Feeding people doesn't solve their problems.' Sam elbowed his friend, who turned to look at Sam with a smirk.

'Maybe not, but it does stop people being hungry and that's a big problem solved.'

The ready friendship between them only reinforced the small-town closeness, and Mick crossed his arms to try and press the tension away. Without leaving town, he'd always be running into Sam. And he couldn't face that possibility. It would just drag the agony out until it broke him.

'True. Plus someone has to look after this one; he's not very good at putting his own needs first.' Sam somehow nailed Mick's character, and from the way Christophe's eyes opened slightly wider, Mick knew he hadn't imagined the care in Sam's voice. Leaving was going to hurt and he wanted to hug himself tight and protect himself from it. He deliberately uncrossed his arms, and took the sandwich from Christophe.

'Thank you for your generosity.'

Christophe smiled. 'Go. Be a hero. God knows we need more of those around here.'

Sam rolled his eyes and waltzed out of the kitchen, with the keys dangling from his fingers.

Mick waved the sandwich towards Christophe. 'I mean it, thank you. It's been a day.'

'A day? Still a few more hours by my counting.' Christophe paused, then winked. 'Seriously, it's fine. Anyone who looks after our fireys during a bushfire is welcome. Please come and eat properly here—on the house—when you have some time.'

'Thank you.' Mick knew he would never take up that offer. He couldn't face eating there alone with the constant reminder of the amazing dinner he'd shared with Sam in the very same place. He knew what he would lose by leaving. And he knew how much it would hurt to stay.

Sam's voice echoed along the short corridor. 'Are you coming? I thought you had to get back to work in a hurry?' The snap in Sam's voice echoed Xavier's and that was it.

'Forget it. I'll get a cab.' He could pay them when he got to the station.

'Don't be ridiculous. You are so determined to go back to work after a traumatic experience, you need someone to care for you.'

Mick growled. 'I don't need you to care for me.' He couldn't owe Sam anything; even contemplating it made his brain blank and he wanted to run far away. People always asked for those debts to be repaid with excessive interest.

'Obviously you do. Besides, there is only one cab in town, and you just sent the driver to hospital with Keerthi.'

'Bert drives the cab? But he's a firefighter.'

'The fireys are volunteers. Given the look of that break, no one is getting a cab around here for months. Just let me drive you.'

'Fine.' Mick obviously had no other option. Exhaustion started to sink in and again his legs wobbled as if they were mush. Sam merely nodded, held the keys up high and pushed the button, scanning the carpark.

'You don't know what car he drives?' Mick apparently had no self-control because he couldn't stop himself chatting with Sam. He automatically tensed, waiting for the derogatory response.

'I take it that means you are coming with me.' Sam's tone was gentle, and Mick's heart skipped a beat. 'And no, I didn't know until I pushed the button, but that old white Toyota four-wheel-drive just beeped, so my guess is that one. Makes sense that Christophe would drive something ordinary and practical. Don't be fooled by his fancy French accent, he's a pretty down-to-earth kind of guy.' Sam chatted happily as he marched towards the vehicle, once again leaving Mick to gape after him. Obviously he had no clue of the argument raging inside Mick's head.

Mick sighed and followed because he needed to get back to the station. He had to follow up with Keerthi and figure out what to do about the ambulance. It might have burned by now; what was the procedure for dealing with that? And there were probably a bunch of other things he needed to organise in case this fire got worse. If they were down to only one ambulance, then he should arrange for back-up from another town. He had his own supervisor's vehicle, but it wasn't kitted out like a proper ambulance. Still—it would make do if needed. It felt good to focus on work. The last thing he wanted to do was say goodbye to Sam. He needed to do it, for his own good, and the doubt swirling around his torso like a herd of bees didn't help at all. A herd? No, a swarm. Damn, he was so tired and confused.

'Stop worrying.' Sam turned the key and the big throaty diesel engine turned over.

'I can't. There's a lot to get sorted out, and we don't know how big this fire is going to get.'

Sam twisted around to reverse out of the carpark. 'We do. That part of the headland only has a limited amount of bush, and not many people live there. It can't jump the river—even at the narrowest part; it's still too wide unless the wind gets a lot stronger.'

'That might happen.'

Sam shook his head, then turned to drive out of the resort towards Marandowie. 'But it's unlikely. I went up the river to see how bad it might get, and I doubt it'll get much worse. It's already burned through the thickest part of the bush. It'll be easier to control once it gets near more open farmland. And the wind is already dying down, which will help.'

'You sound so certain.'

'One of the benefits of having lived here my whole life, I guess.' Sam shrugged one shoulder and Mick stared silently out the front of Christophe's truck.

'How far?'

'Into town? About twenty minutes.'

Mick swallowed back an impatient sigh.

After ten minutes of silence, Sam asked, 'Have you eaten the bread Christophe gave you?'

Mick had forgotten completely about the sandwich he held his in left hand and the mention of it made his tummy rumble. He lifted it up and took a huge bite, mostly for show, but also because he was suddenly hungry. The yeasty fresh bread combined with pâté and brie wasn't what he expected. His taste buds exploded with a hint of herbs and chilli to counter the soft flavours of the cheese, a softness that made his mouth sigh, and he dragged in a deep appreciative breath through his nostrils.

'Christophe is pretty good at his job.' Sam's sly humour settled the worry in Mick's gut and he ate the gorgeous sandwich until they pulled up outside the station. It was too bad that he had to break up with him.

Chapter 14

The next day Sam logged onto SDH and was surprised to see no DMs from Mick. Rather than send him a message, he picked up his phone and rang him. The phone rang out and Mick's voicemail message came on. He waited for the beep.

'Hey, just calling to see if you are okay? Call me back when you can.' As he hung up, his phone vibrated with a text message.

Mick: I can't see you anymore. Dating you hasn't worked out for me. Thanks.

Sam stared unblinking at his phone. After a while his chest hurt and he realised he'd forgotten to breathe. He thought things were good between them, at least until the moment with Mick's scars. But then there was the fire and Sam assumed everything was good now. Mick was leaving him? He was glad he was already sitting down because he wanted to collapse in a puddle.

Sam: Can we talk?
Mick: I don't think that's a good idea.
Sam: I don't want to hurt you.
Mick: You already have.
Sam: Please. Let me fix this.

He waited. And waited. But after a few minutes, it was obvious Mick wasn't going to respond. What now? How do you fix a problem without knowing what it was? He almost googled that, just in case someone on the internet had a solution. Like a Reddit post: *AITA for wanting to know why my boyfriend won't talk about the massive scar on his back?* Sam jumped out of his chair and marched into the tiny lounge room of their cottage. His brother was stretched out on the couch watching some doco on telly.

'Hey Kiet.'

'Yeah?'

'Am I the asshole here?'

Kiet sat up and pressed pause on the remote. 'What?'

'Mick won't talk to me.'

Kiet frowned, then shrugged. 'Maybe he's embarrassed that he needed to be rescued by you. Those paramedic types have a bit of a hero complex.'

'You think?' Sam wasn't sure it had anything to do with that, although Mick had been quite terse in the boat. But he'd put that down to the fact that he was working, that he had two injured people to deal with. No one was in the mood for chit chat yesterday.

'Sure. Has he said anything?'

'No. That's the thing. He doesn't want to talk about it. He just left.'

Kiet's eyes widened. 'What the hell? He can't do that to you.'

'But he did.' Sam's shoulders slumped. The truth hurt and he couldn't find the energy to push it away with a jest. Mick could do whatever he wanted. The timing sucked too. Sam was finally ready to take the next step into a relationship, and he knew he wasn't rushing. They'd spent lots of time together and built a strong friendship before he'd let lust take over. Or so he thought. He rubbed the tight muscle at the base of his skull.

'It's not your fault.'

'I think it might be.'

'No. People leave for their own reasons. It has nothing to do with you.'

Sam rolled his eyes. Bloody brothers, being all concerned about ancient history. 'I'm not worried about that. I know you think I have a complex about people leaving me—'

'Yeah, like Nok, our parents, Lizzy ... Shall I continue?'

Sam gasped. 'No, you shouldn't. Mick is nothing like that. Our parents died. They didn't leave by choice.' The truth was that his parents would never have left if they'd had a choice. They stayed here with him and Kiet and the farm because they loved it here. They died doing the work they loved, and honestly, Papa had never really left. Sam felt his presence occasionally when he was out on the water.

'I know and I'm glad you realise it too.'

Sam tried to smile but it felt like an awkward grimace. 'Besides, you haven't left.'

'I'll always be here.'

'Yeah, taking up all the room on the couch!'

Kiet laughed and for a long moment, they said nothing. 'Do you love him?'

'Who? Mick?'

'Yes. Mick.'

Sam paced around the room. This damned cottage was too small. It had never bothered him before. He'd grown up here, so it just was what it was. He'd never noticed the cramped size until now. 'I don't know. I think I could start to love him.' As soon as the words slipped out, Sam knew they weren't the truth. He did love Mick. If he didn't, he wouldn't be here trying to figure this out. He nearly slapped himself in the head. He shouldn't be *here* trying to sort this out. He should be with Mick. He hadn't needed to chase Lizzy when she left, he'd just let her because it hadn't mattered like this. Mick mattered to him.

'I'll be back.'

'Okay. Take your time.' Kiet pressed play on the remote as if it were the most normal thing in the world for Sam to bolt out of the house, leap into his ute, and drive into Marandowie to grovel at the feet of his, hopefully, boyfriend.

Twenty minutes later, Sam stood at the ambulance station, his heart still racing. Could he claim he was dying of a broken heart? Or was that a touch too dramatic? It felt like it, though. He breathed in deeply, squared his shoulders, flicked his hair off his forehead, and pushed open the door beside the ambulance bay.

'Mick?'

'Sam? What are you doing here?'

'I came to apologise for hurting you.'

Mick scowled. 'I'm at work.'

Sam let out a long slow breath. 'I realise that, and I'm sorry for interrupting.'

Mick didn't say anything, just stared at him with a furrowed brow. Mick's eyes shone with moisture, the only hint that his stare wasn't all about this hard, sharp, rejection.

'Look, I'm here because I don't know where you live. We've only ever met online, at my farm, or like ... at the pub and stuff.' Sam hadn't realised until this moment how imbalanced that was. 'Honestly, I'm not sure if that's a bad reflection on me or you?' He tried to pass off his doubt as a joke, but it fell flat.

'I can't do this now.'

Sam wanted to glare, but it was Mick, and his heart ached at how upset Mick looked. He couldn't find the strength to be angry at him. Mostly he was just confused by Mick's choices and he wanted to bundle him in a hug and hold him tight until everything was better.

'You need to leave.'

Sam swallowed. He straightened his spine and took the biggest risk of his life. 'I love you, Mick. I'm strong enough to cope with your hurt. You can keep pushing me away but I'm your rock. I'll stand strong for you.' His heart pounded, loud in his ears, like a subwoofer vibrating bass notes through his body.

'No.' Mick turned his back and picked up a pen. He didn't write anything, just sat there. Sam swayed on his feet. So much for being an immovable boulder. Sam counted his breaths. In and out. With each breath, the rhythm slowed, and he felt steadier. He'd made it all the way to two hundred and eighty-seven when Mick spun in his chair. Yes! His patience was rewarded. Mick must understand that he'd be there for him.

'Just go.'

'What?'

'Go. I ... I have to work.' Mick turned away again and this time Sam left. If he wasn't wanted, he would do the leaving. He just wished it didn't feel like he was leaving part of his heart behind.

Chapter 15

Two days later, Mick walked out of the session with his therapist completely wrung out. No wonder people didn't go to therapy. This was his third session and it hit him harder than the first two. He was utterly wrecked, every fibre in his body saggy and adrift. This was more exhausting than standing in a river during a bushfire holding an injured fireman. Much more exhausting. He'd cried for an hour until he'd run out of liquid and his eyes were blurred. But now the tears had dried and Maddie's words rang in his head.

'When someone truly loves you, they make sacrifices for you. They put your needs above theirs, and if you love them, you will do the same. A true partnership works in both directions.' The problem with Xavier was that he only loved himself. He had always put himself first. Sam had never done that; just because Mick kept expecting him to behave like Xavier didn't mean that Sam would. He'd really fucked up by assuming Sam would treat him the same. The evidence told him otherwise. One moment in today's therapy session had begun the flood of tears, the moment he'd started to tell Maddie about their conversation at the station a couple of days ago—when he'd ended things with Sam. He'd mentioned how Sam had come to the station to talk to him because he didn't know where he lived, and he'd sobbed until he'd hiccupped. Sam was right—Mick had never invited Sam to his house—and Maddie had simply nodded.

'Do you think that's because you never felt safe when you lived with Xavier? So being at home with someone else is uncomfortable for you?'

He'd argued. 'But—I don't live there anymore. This is a new house. Xavier has never been here. He doesn't know the address.' And neither did Sam. That was the moment Mick knew he loved Sam and he'd ruined everything by not being honest with Sam about his past.

Now he was leaning against his car, slowly breathing in and out, thinking about Sam. Like Maddie said, he hadn't ruined everything forever. His mother's advice about fixing mistakes rang clearly in his mind and chased away his doubts. All he had to do was talk to Sam and hope he understood. He needed to risk being rejected by Sam, to tell his truth, no matter how ugly. He needed to apologise, and then he needed to keep working on himself. It was more than letting himself trust Sam—his stomach flipped over at the thought—it needed ongoing work. It might just be the most difficult thing he'd ever done in his life. Harder than realising Xavier didn't care about him. That was old news, a small emotional spike compared to the way his chest ached and bile made his throat acidic at the very thought of telling Sam the ugly truth.

But Mick realised he wanted Sam more than he was afraid, so he swallowed down the bitterness and went through the motions of getting into his car, putting on his seatbelt, and turning on the engine. The radio belted out the latest song by Thelma Plum and he nodded along. The soulful pop tunes helped settle his stomach and he ran through the list of things he needed to pick up from town on his way out to Sam's farm.

An hour later, he was driving along the gum-tree-lined driveway at Sam's oyster farm and a sense of homecoming filled his bones. He'd always felt safe here, a place where people listened to him and didn't dismiss his thoughts as less important than theirs. On the surface, it was why he always came here and didn't invite Sam to his place. He blinked and shook his head as he recalled their discussion about the domestic violence victims he treated at work. He hadn't known it then, but he'd been the abused guy who kept returning, and it had taken Sam's no-nonsense approach for him to realise the depth of hurt Xavier had caused. Going to therapy was the second step in healing himself—the first had been admitting Sam was right and he needed help. He parked the car and grabbed the package off the passenger seat. With a slight tremble in his fist, he knocked on the door.

'Come in.'

Mick had planned to say something sensible about how he knew that love wouldn't solve his problems. He had to sort that out himself, and he wanted to do it for Sam. Love made him want to be better. But everything fled as he stared at Sam standing in the kitchen washing dishes.

'Hi.' Sam waved a wet hand.

Mick cleared his throat. 'I brought you a key to my house.'

'Excuse me?'

'Sorry. Let me start again.' Mick dropped the package on the table, scrubbed his hands through his hair, and pressed the heel of his hands against the corner of his eyes.

'Sure. Hi.'

'Hi.' Mick sighed. 'I had a whole speech planned, but damn, you are so bloody gorgeous, Sam. I can't remember any of it.'

Sam raised one eyebrow, then dropped his gaze back to the task of washing dishes.

'So here goes.' Mick sucked in a deep refreshing breath, filling his lungs, and let it out slowly. 'About a year ago, I went to a job at a factory fire, and as I was helping someone, a partially burned piece of wall fell on me. I spent ages in hospital getting skin grafts and stuff.' He waved his hand at his back.

'I'm not repulsed by your scars, Mick.'

'I know. It's not you.' He held up his palms. 'Remember I said an ex introduced me to SDH because it was a queer hook-up platform?' Mick dropped his hands. He didn't wait for an answer, just barrelled on. 'Xavier used it to cheat on me. That's how I found out about the game. I started playing to keep an eye on him. But what has that to do with the fire, you might ask?'

Sam hummed and Mick fiddled with the cuff of his shirt.

'Awkward phrasing, I know.'

'It's fine, Mick. You don't have to tell me if you aren't comfortable.'

Mick swallowed. 'But I do. When the fire happened, I was living in an apartment in Sydney with Xavier. Yes, even though he cheated on me, and stuff. I was a fool; charmed by him, I guess. Anyway, after the fire, I didn't hear from him. And when I rang him, he said he needed to visit his sister and I wasn't good for his image anymore.'

'His image?' Sam's voice rose slightly.

Mick held up his palm. 'It's a mess. Xavier had a fancy job in government, some kind of adviser, and he thought that having a paramedic hero as his boyfriend was good for his image.'

'And you let him say that to you?'

'Yeah. Look, I know it reflects badly on me. I'm seeing a therapist to help me figure it out.' Mick wished it was as easy as stepping sideways and watching the heavy weight on his shoulders fall to the ground and splinter into pieces, but he knew he would have to chip away at it until it transformed into something new. A sculpture crafted out of marble.

'Good. Because this Xavier person has obviously messed you up a lot.'

Mick nodded. 'And that's my cue to apologise. I'm sorry that my cheating ex-boyfriend screwed with my ability to see good sense. I know you didn't mean to hurt me when you touched my scars. It's just that—'

'Xavier told you they repulsed him? Did I guess right?'

'Yes.'

Sam grabbed a tea towel and scrubbed his hands dry. 'I am not Xavier. Shit, that name. It sounds like the name some rich trophy wife would call out in a sing-song voice at a park. "Xavier! Xavier, don't get your socks dirty now!"'

Unbidden laughter flooded Mick's body until he was doubled over with it, as if all the tension and emotion he'd been holding in had been released. 'Oh God, that's so true. Now I feel sorry for any kid given that name.'

'It's the kind of name you give one of those poor squashed-up-nose pug dogs.'

Mick laughed again and shook his head helplessly. 'Poor things. So over-bred they can't breathe.' He hadn't expected Sam's quirky humour—somehow in all this introspection, he'd forgotten the easy way they chatted to each other. It didn't set out to charm him or expect an ego-stroking response from him. It simply was there. No expectations, no pleasant phrasing intended to undermine Mick's confidence. He breathed out, a long shuddering flood of air.

'It's cruel.' Sam spoke in unison with him, and they both stood in silence for a few minutes. Now Mick could see it, the difference was stark. Sam was honest, refreshing, funny. Perfectly himself without guile. And damn, Mick wanted him so much. So much that his skin began to warm up and his blood began to pulse in anticipation.

'Sam, you are so cute and funny and kind. And nothing at all like Xavier, which to be honest is the greatest compliment. I fell in love with you from the moment we sat in the pub and your hair flopped over your forehead. My love has grown every time we talked, online and IRL, until it was so strong that it completely freaked me out. I'm so sorry I overreacted and pushed you away. Please...' Mick picked up the package from the table. 'Please, have a key to my house.'

'Thank you. Mick. I'd love to have a key to your house. The address would be good too.'

'Sam!'

'I'm teasing. I need to apologise too. I pushed you too hard. I should have waited until you were ready to talk about it.'

'No. It's okay. I needed that shove so I didn't keep wallowing in self-pity.'

'It's not self-pity when you've been emotionally abused by someone. You are allowed to be cautious with who you trust.'

Mick smiled. 'I trust you. I think I always have, by instinct, even when I didn't know I did. And when you and your damned boat arrived in the fire, I realised how much I trusted you. The fire reminded me of the other fire, and I—'

'Yeah?'

'I guess I assumed that you wouldn't stick around for me. Wait. It was a bad assumption.' Mick laughed, a hard bark as he realised something.

'What?'

'When we first met in the pub, you said you wanted to go slowly because you'd just broken up with someone and you didn't want to rush in and rebound. That we were friends and that mattered to you. I was wrong. That was the moment I think I started to fall in love with you. You were so confident in knowing what you wanted, and I had run away from my old life without even understanding what I'd run from.'

'I must be a good actor, then. I wasn't confident at all. Lizzy had messed with my sense of worth.' Sam glanced up at the ceiling. 'Look at the pair of us. Both screwed up by our exes, unable to trust ourselves to start again.'

Mick grinned. 'Maybe that was us when we first met but look at us now. I want to build a life with you, Sam. I love you.'

Sam walked around the kitchen bench and wrapped his arms around Mick. 'I love you and want that too. I think I've waited long enough.'

'For?'

Sam kissed him, and everything was right in the world for the first time in days. 'To ask you into my bedroom. I've waited and taken my time, and I'm ready. Come with me.' Sam stepped out of the hug and held Mick's hand. He started to walk to his bedroom and lust rushed through Mick's veins. Lust that was warmer than usual, as if the sharp needy edges were rounded by love.

Epilogue

Mick: I love you. Now start packing.

Sam smiled and logged into SDH instead of packing. They were heading down to Sydney for Mardi Gras after Mick's shift. Mick wouldn't be online unless he was neglecting his job—something he wouldn't do because he was dedicated—and Sam sipped a glass of water to try and wash away the flush of disappointment that came from that. They'd split their time equally between Mick's place in town and Sam's tiny bedroom, but neither really worked. Sam didn't appreciate having to get up even earlier to get to work on time. Staying at the farm would be best, but there really wasn't enough space in their cottage for four adults. A notification for a DM hovered, and Sam clicked on it.

Velebit: Since you are named after an oyster, and I'm named after a mountain range, I think we should name our new joint venture on here 'Sheep's Testicles'.

Sam barked out a laugh. *Crassostrea: No. If you must, we could use the actual euphemism 'mountain oysters', but no.*

He didn't expect a reply. Mick wouldn't be back online for a few more hours. Sam spent an hour doing some trades on SDH, and then logged out of the game to spend some time searching through all his photos to find the perfect one to give to Mick. Finding one that wasn't a shark and that showed off the farm nicely was trickier than he'd first assumed. Too many of his photos focused on the fish themselves, without worrying too much about the backdrop. He planned to upload the best one to an online print company, get it printed onto canvas, and delivered to Mick's place.

Kiet entered the room at the same time as he knocked.

'Bro, I could've been naked,' Sam protested. Ever since Zoe had moved in, Sam had been much more careful with entering Kiet's room, not wanting to accidentally upset Zoe.

'I've seen it all before. Have you packed yet?'

Sam laughed. 'I take it you and Zoe are keen to have the house to yourselves for a few days.' He'd be the same in the reverse situation.

'Yes. Go and enjoy the Mardi Gras with your man.' Kiet's smile was broad and Sam found himself grinning back.

'We've done alright, haven't we?'

'We have.'

'About the cottage situation...' Sam wasn't sure how to broach this subject with his brother. It was something he'd chatted about with Mick over the last couple of days. Kiet raised his eyebrows and waited, so Sam just blurted it out. 'Mick and I thought we should invest in building a new house on the farm.' They also had bigger plans. Mick was keen to hand his job over to Keerthi and spend less time as a paramedic. He had grand plans to invest some of that time into a health retreat, bed-and-breakfast style, business in one of the paddocks overlooking Rainbow Cove.

'For you two?'

'And you guys. This cottage is past its use-by date, and Mick has designed a new version of the cottage that has three wings all connected by a wrap-around balcony to take advantage of the view.' Sam's soon to be fiancé—assuming Mick said yes when he asked him at Mardi Gras tomorrow—was a brilliant amateur architect. It hadn't surprised Sam when they'd first discussed it, because all the signs were there in the way he played SDH.

'Three wings?'

'Yes. A small office building at one end, where clients can meet us if they need, or staff can work if we expand. A middle building that is big enough for you and Zoe, and any kids if you have them, and a smaller building at the other end for Mick and me.'

Kiet nodded. 'I like that concept. We'd still be together, but we'd have our own space.'

'Yes. I need to be here for work. Whenever I stay at Mick's I have to get up too early and then I'm tired by lunchtime. And Mick can live anywhere.'

'How would we fund this?'

Sam shook his head. 'I'm not sure. It's just an idea at this stage, but you know, like, Zoe is an accountant, so she'd have more clue than me. I guess we'd have to sort out a financing arrangement, with some of it paid by the farm, and some paid by Zoe and Mick. I reckon we can all work something out.'

'Let me talk to Zoe.' Kiet started to leave, then looked over his shoulder, 'And get on with that packing. Mick will be here soon.'

Sam laughed, and grabbed his suitcase from under his bed. 'I'm going. Gee, you'd think you were keen to be alone with your missus or something!'

Kiet's faint blush made the teasing worthwhile. Besides, the sooner they built a bigger place, the better. It'd be great to have some actual storage, and he could decorate the office with some of his photos. The combination of art and architecture would make their health retreat a unique reflection of their hobbies. Sam had just finishing packing his bag when there was a light knock on the door. He straightened and turned to see Mick, his Mick, standing in the doorway.

'How many times have I told you that you don't need to knock? My room is your room.'

Mick grinned. 'I see you left packing until the very last moment.' He stepped into Sam's open arms and kissed him. 'My gorgeous messy Sam. You are a delight and I love you.'

'I love you too.' Sam wrapped his arms around Mick's waist and pulled him even closer. 'It took me ages to figure it out, and I want you to know that it's completely true. I love you.'

'Shall we go and celebrate?'

Sam kissed Mick on the forehead. 'Absolutely. Let's get ourselves to Mardi Gras and show the world our love.'

Mick picked up Sam's suitcase in one hand, and with the other, he held Sam's hand as if it were the most precious of his belongings. Together they walked out towards Mick's car and a future together. Sam had found everything he needed: a sense of understanding about himself, and the love of his life with Mick. They could build a life together, and if Nok ever returned to Rainbow Cove, they'd be here with open arms for her. If she didn't, Sam would cope, knowing his lover and best friend would stand beside him no matter what the world threw at them next. There was no way he'd be able to wait to ask Mick to marry him. Sam had become comfortable with his own impulsiveness and already the ring in his pocket was starting to burn a hole in it. It was time to let the ring be free and hook the two of them together forever.

'Hey Mick?'

'Yes?'

'Will you marry me?' Sam held up the ring and Mick laughed.

'Yes. A million times, yes. I knew you couldn't wait until Mardi Gras.'

Nothing could break the smile on Sam's face. 'You knew?'

'My darling Sam. You measured my finger a week ago while I was snoozing.'

Sam rolled his eyes. 'You didn't say anything.'

'No, because I did the same the day before.' Mick leaned into the car, then stood up, holding a small box. 'See. Now come on, we need to get moving to make it to Mardi Gras on time.'

Sam jumped off the porch and opened the box Mick held. The ring was a gorgeous titanium band with sharks engraved into the surface in a curling wave, as if they chased each other around his finger. 'OMG, that's beautiful.'

'Marry me?'

'Yes.' There was nothing more to be said. Sam wanted this as much as Mick did. The future of Rainbow Cove looked brighter than the glare of the summer sun off the water.

Thanks for reading *His Christmas Pride.* I hope you enjoyed it.

If you liked this book, here are my other titles: **His Christmas Pearl,** *Merindah Park, Making Her Mark,* and **Two Hearts Healing** and **Racetrack Royalty.** You might also like **To Charm a Bluestocking, In Pursuit of a Bluestocking** and **The Heart of a Bluestocking.**

Sign up to our newsletter ***romance.com.au/newsletter/*** and find out about new releases, must-read series and ***ebook deals*** at romance.com.au.

Reviews can help readers find books, and I am grateful for all honest reviews. Thank you for taking the time to let others know what you've read, and what you thought.

Share your reading experience on:
Facebook
Instagram
romance.com.au

Bestselling Titles by Escape Publishing...

Discover more in the Rainbow Cove Christmas series...

One gourmet party. Four potential couples. The taste of love?

His Christmas Feast

Nora James

After his girlfriend runs off with another man, French chef Christophe Duval swears to stay away from women. That all changes when his sexy neighbour Emily Brighton turns up at the lavish Christmas party he throws at his country home in Marandowie. The trouble is, Emily is the queen of mixed signals and Christophe is along for a rollercoaster ride like no other. Will he ever understand her? Will he ever tame her? Or will the fence they set out to build between their two properties keep them apart for good?

Her Christmas Kisses
Susanne Bellamy

Devastated by her parents' divorce and the impending sale of the family restaurant, Flick Ardmore is determined to find the money to buy the restaurant. She doesn't expect to find herself stranded in Rainbow Cove with no car, no work, and no prospect of success.

Xander McIntyre, owner of the luxury Rainbow Cove Resort, is a workaholic developer with a looming deadline hindered by the arrival of his young special needs sister, Jenny.

When Flick connects with Jenny, it seems like the perfect solution to both their problems—if only Flick and Xander can ignore the undeniable spark between them. Or will their building attraction cause more problems than it solves?

Her Christmas Homecoming
Shirley Wine

For singer, Marta Field, her return home is bittersweet. Difficult as it is to put her mother into care and clear out her family home so it can go on the market, the hardest challenge is meeting up with Joe Marshall, the man she loved and left behind.

Joe is older now and grounded in the soil of his home town, but Marta can see no long-term future for herself in Rainbow Cove. Besides, she's never forgiven Joe for giving up on their shared dreams. Will the magic of Christmas help these star-crossed lovers find their way back to each other?

His Christmas Pearl
Renée Dahlia

The last thing Kiet Viravaidya wants to do on Christmas Day is deliver oysters from his farm to a party that he's not invited to. But duty calls-the party is being hosted by Christophe, a chef who is a regular client, and having been stung by embezzlement, Kiet's business needs the money. Kiet doesn't want to talk to people, and history has taught him he can't trust anyone, especially not the gorgeous stranger in a ridiculous Christmas dress with dangling Santa earrings.

Zoe Russell loves Christmas but thanks to her family, the last couple of Christmases haven't been much fun. When she's invited to Christophe's Christmas party, she leaps to say yes. Zoe spies Kiet shucking oysters in the kitchen, and something about his competent hands draws her to him. She wants to know more about him, and as a forensic accountant, she can't resist the thrill of figuring out who is embezzling from his business.

It seems like the perfect reason to spend time together.

His Christmas Escape
Shona Husk

One gourmet party. Six potential couples. The taste of love?

Nico De Luca has been doing his best to keep his family together and off the street since he was sixteen. Everyone thinks he's doing such a good thing, but they never care about the cost to him. With his stepfather fresh out of jail ... again ... trouble is brewing.

Coming home after travelling is always bittersweet for Jade Russell. She loves seeing her sister and friends, but her parents have made it very clear she's not welcome. Christmas is full of fake happiness and spending money on junk people don't want. She sees it in the parents' eyes in her job as an elf taking photos with Santa.

When Nico meets Jade in her elf uniform, he is enchanted. When they meet again at a Rainbow Cove Christmas lunch, he realises Jade is out of his league. She knows what she's doing with her life. She has a life. Following Jade makes stepping off the path easy and, before he knows it, freedom is within Nico's grasp. But if he leaves, he can never come back...